Love Finds You™

IN

Frost

MINNESOTA

Love Finds You™
IN
Frost
MINNESOTA

FIC
BAER
2013

JUDY BAER

summerside
PRESS™

New York

Love Finds You in Frost, Minnesota

ISBN-10: 0-8249-3435-0
ISBN-13: 978-0-8249-3435-4

Published by Summerside Press, an imprint of Guideposts
16 East 34th Street
New York, New York 10016
SummersidePress.com
Guideposts.org

Summerside Press™ is an inspirational publisher offering fresh, irresistible books to uplift the heart and engage the mind.

Distributed by Ideals Publications, a Guideposts company
2630 Elm Hill Pike, Suite 100
Nashville, TN 37214

Guideposts, Ideals, and *Summerside Press* are registered trademarks of Guideposts.

The town depicted in this book is a real place, but all names are fictional except that of Charles S. Frost (May 31, 1856–December 11,1931), the architect after whom Frost is named. Any resemblances to any people living or dead are purely accidental.

Scripture references are from the following sources: The Holy Bible, New International Version®, NIV®. Copyright © 1973, 1978, 1984, 2011 by Biblica, Inc.™ Used by permission of Zondervan. All rights reserved worldwide. The Holy Bible, English Standard Version® (ESV), copyright © 2001 by Crossway Bibles, a publishing ministry of Good News Publishers. Used by permission.

Cover and interior design by Müllerhaus Publishing Group, Mullerhaus.net

Printed and bound in the United States of America
10 9 8 7 6 5 4 3 2 1

Dedication

....

For Josie, Keillor, and Quentin—Merry Christmas

Acknowledgments
....

Kudos to the real Frost, Minnesota, for being
such a tidy and charming small town!

Frost, Minnesota

THE TINY TOWN OF FROST IS SITUATED IN SOUTHERN Minnesota. With fewer than 200 residents, it has a post office, library, several agricultural businesses, and three Lutheran churches. Frost was named for Charles S. Frost (1856–1931), an architect from Chicago who designed The Depot in Minneapolis/St. Paul, Chicago's Navy Pier, the Navy Pier Terminal Building, and numerous other landmarks.

The town of Frost was platted in 1888, and the post office began operation in 1899. The majority of the settlers were Norwegian, and the town's residents still enjoy Scandinavian traditions such as church *lutefisk* dinners at Christmastime. Though Frost is very real and lovely, the places and characters portrayed in this book are not. Still, I fell in love with the place during my visit, and I like to imagine all the wonderful people who must live there.

—Judy Baer

Chapter One

Merry Blake straightened the gold angel at the top of the Christmas tree and stood back to inspect it. She had the same curly blonde fluff of hair as the angel staring benevolently down at her, the same green eyes, and the same perpetually happy expression, as if Christmas joy were etched into her soul.

Twigs Merry had collected and sprayed gold glinted from between the branches of the fourteen-foot white pine adorned with metallic gold bows, balls, and ornaments. This was her finest yet, she decided, which said a lot, considering that she'd decorated more than a hundred and fifty trees in the past five years. Yes indeed, Merry's Christmas Boutique was looking better than ever.

She checked on the fragrant spiced cider in the electric urn near the spiral staircase to see that it was warm. Her part-time helper would head for it first thing when she arrived. Abby Phillips was almost as crazy about Christmas—and cider—as Merry.

The door opened and a cascade of chimes exploded, the motion-activated reindeer began to play "Rudolph the Red-Nosed Reindeer," and a raucous movement-sensitive Santa chortled "Ho, ho, ho."

Upon hearing the auditory explosion, Merry turned to greet Abby. She was startled to see not her friend but a tall, broad-shouldered, elegantly dressed man with thick dark hair, brown eyes, and a frown that etched deep furrows in his high, intelligent forehead. He appeared to be a few years older than she, thirty-five to her twenty-eight, perhaps. Snow lay sprinkled across the shoulders of his black wool coat, and a gust of icy wind followed him inside. She shivered a bit in her Mrs. Claus red velvet skirt and fur-trimmed blouse.

"Welcome to Frost. May I help you?" Strangers didn't often come through the streets of Frost, a tiny town in southern Minnesota inhabited by a large percentage of people with Norwegian and German heritages—except now, of course, at Christmastime, when her boutique drew people from as far away as Minneapolis, St. Paul, and even Sioux Falls, South Dakota.

"What *is* this?" The question was far from friendly, but the fellow's scowling demeanor didn't conceal his handsome features. His coat fell open to reveal black trousers and a cashmere V-neck sweater with a pristine white shirt beneath.

"This is Merry's Christmas Boutique. Frost's one and only Christmas store. We open on Black Friday and close January seventh, right after our clearance sale." Merry smoothed her skirt and hoped she didn't have straw from the Nativity sets in her hair. "Are you looking for a special Christmas gift? Stocking stuffers?"

He stared at her as if the synapses in her brain were made of peppermint bark. Disapproval oozed from every attractive pore. "Stocking stuffers? What kind of nonsense is that?"

"Nonsense? Don't you like Christmas?" If not, what was he doing here in Frost, the town that had fully embraced Merry's marketing concept and turned itself into a tiny Christmas village for almost two months every year?

"Has this place gone completely nuts?" Icicles dripped from his words.

"Candied pecans, perhaps," she said through gritted teeth, determined not to allow him to fill the shop with his negativity. "They're one of my best sellers. Would you like to try some?"

He ignored her. "Frost is nothing like the last time I was here at Christmas. Now there are Santas on every corner, reindeer and sleighs perched on every rooftop, and a weird talking Christmas tree by the post office that doesn't shut up! The only thing that makes any sense is the life-sized Nativity at the church."

"That's my favorite too, but people think of Santas, reindeer, and elves at this time of year as well." She snapped her fingers. "That reminds me—did you see elves as you drove through town? Abby's husband, Charley Phillips, was supposed to put them up—hanging out of the trees, peeking from behind rocks, and the like. It's very clever, and the children love them."

His scowl deepened, and he looked as if he could use a little sugar boost.

Merry hurried to get him a cup of cider. She thrust it into his hand, and he stared at it suspiciously.

"It's not poison, for goodness' sake! Drink it. You look as though your blood sugar is dropping."

"Who are you?" he asked, after a gulp of cider. "Where did you come from? The North Pole?"

Merry beamed at him, pleased with the suggestion. "I'm Merry Blake. I've lived in Frost for five years. I teach morning kindergarten in Blue Earth and work afternoons and evenings here, at least through the holidays. I substitute teach the rest of the time."

He continued to gape at her as if she'd just arrived on the Polar Express, so she continued. "I've always loved Christmas, so when I had a chance to buy this place—for little or nothing, I might add—I grabbed it. It's the perfect Christmas house. Every year I turn it into a boutique. I also do high teas and luncheons for groups of ladies and act as an occasional bed-and-breakfast for people who come to town to visit. I had no idea the store would take off like this. Now I earn more in two months than I do teaching. I'd never quit that, however. I love little kids."

She saw his eyes glazing and bit her lip. She was so happy with how things had turned out that it was hard for her *not* to talk about it. Teaching children, a lovely home, and the opportunity to dwell on Christmas all year long and to seek out people to enjoy it with—what could be better? Because she was an only child of only children, big family Christmases were the stuff of magazine covers and store windows until she began to make her own.

Christmas had always been a lonely time for her. No siblings or cousins for whom to purchase gifts, no aunts or uncles to prepare for, and certainly no great anticipation about the presents under the tree. Her parents were practical people who gave her things like socks, school clothes, and money. Despite their pragmatic approach to life, she missed them terribly. When they'd died unexpectedly in a car accident, her only family left was a great-aunt. She pushed away the thought of the one thing that would make Christmas perfect—family, people to call her own.

Though she could never replace her parents, she had a lot of good friends, both male and female. There were an especially large number of male friends who'd like to be invited to her house for Christmas, but for some of them that was almost equivalent to a marriage proposal—and she was in no hurry to rush into a permanent institution with any of them. Already she'd decided to invite her lonely neighbor Hildy over for the holidays.

Only when nights got long and she ached to talk to someone other than her red-and-white border collie, Peppermint, and the butterscotch-colored cat she'd named Eggnog did she feel an emptiness in her life. She had specific, unbending requirements for a mate. Whomever she married would have to love Christmas as much as she. That was nonnegotiable. And, naturally, he would be a Christian.

She hummed as she took the cup from her visitor's hand, refilled it, and handed it back to him. She picked up a plate of cookies. "Something to eat? Spritz cookies, pecan tartlets, and macaroons. There are also caramel peanut clusters, peppermint bark, birds' nests, and divinity. My mother taught me how to make the divinity. It's tricky, you know. I don't like it when it's soft and melts into those puddles. . . ." Merry hesitated when he didn't respond. She was doing it again—rambling on about Christmas.

Her guest held up his hand as if to stop her. "What are you doing here?"

Merry studied him. He looked fine—more than fine, actually—but he was certainly behaving oddly.

"I told you. I live here." She spoke slowly, as if to a misbehaving child. "This is my home. This is my store."

"In Frost?"

The least he could do was look around and see the lovely selection of Christmas items on display, she thought impatiently. "Of course in Frost!" She narrowed her green eyes and set the pretty bow of her mouth in a moue. "Perhaps I should ask what *you* are doing here." She hoped Abby would arrive soon. She was beginning to be uncomfortable with his odd behavior.

"I own Frost."

Merry felt her eyes widen.

He saw her reaction and amended his statement. "I don't own *all* of it, of course, just a *lot* of it."

"What is your name?" Merry clutched the cell phone in her pocket, ready to dial for help.

"My name is Jonathan Frost. My great-grandfather was a cousin of the man after whom this town was named, Charles S. Frost, an architect from Chicago. Apparently he came to see the place that carried his family name, liked it, and settled here. I'm named after my great-grandfather, Jonathan, but my . . . someone in my family called me Jack, and it stuck."

Jack Frost had just walked into her store? This was too good to be true!

Merry hardly registered the part about the town's founder. Jack Frost was here in Frost! She could have an autograph party and get him to sign the framed prints of the photos of morning hoarfrost on the windows that she'd taken last winter. Wouldn't that be fun? She could serve White Christmas, her favorite coconut cake, and . . .

Wait a minute. Had he just said he *owned* the town of Frost?

"How could that be?" Merry couldn't keep the skepticism out of her voice. "You own this town?"

"Bits and pieces, apparently. And a lot of land outside of town. My father passed away recently, and it wasn't until the reading of his will that I discovered that Dad had inherited the property in Frost. It's been in the family for four generations."

Merry tried to digest this bit of information.

"Dad rarely mentioned his great-grandfather, who was gone long before I was born." The young Mr. Frost tugged absently at his ear. "I assume that when the property came to Dad, whoever was taking care of things concerning Frost was dead and gone."

Merry thought of the way she pulled together her own income piecemeal. If Mr. Frost's family could overlook profits and returns like that, they must be very well to do.

Mr. Frost had the grace to look a bit sheepish. "Our family has always had plenty of money. I'm sure it wasn't a big deal to him."

Merry edged her way to the dining room table, set with Spode Christmas china, red napkins, poinsettias, and green placemats. Red-and-white peppermints graced the tabletop, and large teddy bears sat in three of the chairs as if waiting for lunch.

She gestured for Jack to sit down, got more cider for both of them, and put the cookies on the table between them. "So this was all news to you? I thought you said you'd been to Frost before."

"It was a long time ago. One of my grandfather's sisters actually lived in this very house."

"And now it's mine."

"Obviously." His expression grew distant, as if he were in another place and time. "When we visited, I used to crawl through the little door in my aunt's closet that leads to the attic. There were old toys up there, clothes, hats, even a dressmaker's dummy and a civil war uniform. It was rather magical for a little kid."

"It's all still there," Merry said softly. "I didn't have the heart to get rid of it. It felt as though I'd be taking the heart out of the house if I disposed of those things."

He looked surprised, a pleasant change from the perpetual frown he'd been wearing.

"You can look through the attic if you want."

The offer obviously startled him. "It's yours now."

"It belongs to the house. You're part of the house's history. It's okay with me."

She saw his posture soften, then stiffen again, as if he'd been tempted by her offer and then changed his mind. He drummed his fingers on the peppermint-themed tabletop.

"Thank you, but I think there are more important things to do while I'm here, like sort out the mess my father left me."

"How long do you plan to be here?"

"As long as it takes."

"To do what?"

"To interview the people who worked the property, to see exactly how much of this town and the land around it I actually own. And, if I'm lucky, to get this ridiculous bogus Christmas spectacle pruned down to size. I hate the gimmicky thing the holiday has become." Then he seemed to realize what he'd said and how it must have sounded to Merry.

She felt as though she might have to pick up her jaw off the plate in front of her.

Jack Frost wanted to shut down Christmas!

* * * * *

He might as well have landed in Oz or Alice's Wonderland, Jack thought. Apparently the eccentric nature of this entire trip was just beginning. He'd thought it bad enough when he stopped at the county courthouse and discovered that nothing was as clear-cut about the property he'd inherited as he hoped it would be. And now this.

The little town he recalled from his childhood had been turned into a Christmas cash cow, and it turned his stomach. He had little tolerance for any Christmas celebrations other than church, and this was beyond garish. It reminded him of New York when the giant tree was lit in Rockefeller Center, and the skaters looked like toys gliding on a mirror.

She was staring at him, he realized, with something that bordered on alarm. He could hardly blame her. Christmas and its memories always had this effect on him. But enough about that. He shook himself free of his thoughts. He needed to get back to Blue Earth.

"I'd better go," he said awkwardly. "Thanks . . ."

He backed out the door, closed it softly to prevent the musical riot from starting again, and escaped to the refuge of his rented BMW.

Against his better judgment, Jack took the turn that led him to the center of town.

Elves were everywhere, peeking over stumps, out of trees, and from behind snow banks.

He hoped he woke up from this nightmare soon.

Chapter Two

Merry, preoccupied, was still staring at the front door when Abby entered.

"Hey, kiddo! What's up?" Abby bounced in with the enthusiasm that usually matched Merry's own, pulled off her stocking cap, and revealed a pixie haircut filled with static electricity. She had light brown hair, gray eyes, and a big smile that revealed a slight overlap in her two front teeth.

"I thought we could unpack more decorations and set up an extra tree in the kitchen. I found some incredible new ribbon when I was in Minneapolis. Wait till you see it. I—Merry, what's wrong?" Abby stopped chattering and peered at her friend. "Are you okay? You're pale as a sheet!"

"I've just seen a ghost," Merry whispered. "The really bad spirit in *A Christmas Carol*. I saw Christmas Future."

"There are no ghosts, Merry, you know that."

"Then this one was a living, breathing nightmare. He wants to cancel Christmas!"

It took some prodding on Abby's part to get the entire story out of Merry—Jack Frost's arrival, his ownership of much of Frost, his dismay at its holiday flavor, and his suggestion they needed to tone things down in the Christmas decoration department. She left out the words he'd used to describe his thoughts. *Ridiculous. Gimmicky.*

"Why does he care?" Abby demanded. "It doesn't have anything to do with him. He hasn't been here since he was a child, and now he breezes in and wants to change things?"

"He didn't discover that his father had inherited property here until the man's will was read," Merry said. "Now that it's come to him, I suppose he thinks he's responsible and needs to do something about it."

"Leave it alone, that's what I say," Abby said, scowling. "We've been just fine until now. Why fix what's not broken? Until you started this store and the rest of the town picked up on this Christmas village theme, it was just like all the other little towns around here. You are the one who helped Frost! Because of your advertisements, people come from miles and miles around to do their Christmas shopping.

"You're practically an industry around here! What about the man who carves wooden Nativity sets or the ladies who knit kitchen dishcloths to sell at the boutique?" Abby crossed her arms over her chest and scowled. "How *dare* he breeze in here and ruin things for us?"

"I don't know if he's going to ruin things," Merry said weakly. "What he actually said was that he was going to get 'this bogus Christmas spectacle pruned down to size.'"

"Like that's not ruining things? Oh, please! What are you going to do about it, Merry?"

"Me? Why am I the one to do something?"

"Because you're the one who brought the fun of Christmas back to Frost. You believe that we should never forget it is Christ's birthday, but you want us to celebrate with that in mind. I've heard you say it a million times. 'There's much more joy in the season when you know its Reason.' You've got your head on straight about Christmas, Merry. If he actually tries to change things, you have to confront him."

"Maybe I have gone overboard, Abby. It could be a hang-up with me. I have the Christmas crazies."

"You felt you were missing something special, and you created a way to provide it for yourself and others. There's nothing wrong with that."

Merry nodded but didn't say more. She would have to run this by her neighbor. Hildy, an original resident of Frost, had moved here from Minneapolis to live out her days in the home she'd grown up in. She usually had wise and sensible advice when Merry asked for it. She needed someone clearheaded to help her sort it out. Then customers began to arrive and swept every other thought from Merry's mind.

After Abby had left for the evening, Merry put the *Closed* sign on the door and meandered to the bookcase. She pulled out the photo album in which she'd recorded the birth and growth of Merry's Christmas Boutique.

The house had been a mess when she got it, and she'd sometimes regretted selling her parents' home in Minneapolis. Snapshots of ragged holes in the walls revealed ancient lath and plaster. The plumbing was a tangle of rusting pipes, and the un-caulked windows let heat from the inefficient old furnace escape into the out of doors. The beautiful hardwood floors had been nicked and stained with ancient and disgusting spills. There were birds' nests in one of the bedrooms and signs of a raccoon in the basement. It had been backbreaking work, but Merry, with a lot of local help, had turned the place into a point of pride for Frost.

Now this house was not only her home but also her business and her refuge. She knew it would have been nearly impossible to build a Christmas boutique in the Twin Cities of Minneapolis and St. Paul with the savings she had. It didn't sit well with her that Mr. Jack Whoever-He-Was Frost had arrived on her doorstep determined to change the things she loved.

Stomach churning with anxiety, Merry put down the album and picked up her Bible. It opened to Hebrews, and she knew immediately the verse she needed to read. It was in the thirteenth chapter, second verse. *"Do not neglect to show hospitality to strangers, for thereby some have entertained angels unawares."*

Jack Frost, an angel? She couldn't picture it. Neither was she willing to ignore God's Word. Sometimes it was just harder to obey than other times.

With a fresh cup of green tea by her side, Merry opened another book from her shelf, a book on the myths and legends surrounding Christmas.

Jack Frost: an exemplification of cold and frost, a variation on Old Man Winter. He is the one supposedly responsible for the color changes in autumn foliage, cold fingers and toes, and the fern frost designs on windowpanes in winter. Jack Frost is often portrayed as a disturbing mischief-maker.

That was a pretty good description of the Jack Frost she'd met this afternoon—a troublemaker. Sighing, she got up to stoke the fire.

Flames licked upward from the logs and snapped and crackled red-orange when she prodded the fragrant-smelling birch. She hung the poker back among the fireplace tools and stood there warming her hands. It was cold tonight. She returned to the book of Christmas lore again and continued to read.

Jack Frost is normally happy-go-lucky and cheerful unless provoked. Then, in some legends, he kills his victims by covering them with snow.

She groaned and sat back down in her chair.

A naughty sprite. A very naughty one. Was there an omen in this?

She was grateful when the phone rang. She wanted to quit replaying her conversation with Jack in her mind.

"It's a Merry Christmas at Merry's Christmas Boutique. How may I help you?"

"Hi, Merry, it's Zeke."

"Hey, Zeke! What's up? Are you working late tonight?" She and Zeke had been friends ever since she'd moved to the area. They'd gone out a few times before they decided that, for them at least, friendship was more important than dating. He worked for a bank in Blue Earth, and he'd given her wise counsel about starting her business. During that time she'd been in desperate need of a big brother. Zeke filled the bill nicely. God had given her someone to watch out for her. Their friendship was one of the best parts of having moved to Frost.

"A little. Are you busy?"

"Just winding down. These are hectic days for me— holding Christmas teas, keeping the store open, refilling stock, all that. I'm so grateful that I have Abby to help me."

"Oh." There was a momentary silence on the other end of the line.

"Zeke? What is it?"

"You just answered the question I'd planned to ask you when I called. I, of all people, should know how it is for you at this time of year."

"Why don't you ask me the question before you decide what my answer is?"

"There's a note on my desk asking me to call you and see if you'd be willing to rent out a room tonight. This individual didn't realize every hotel in a forty-mile radius is filled with high school basketball players and their families for the holiday tournaments.

"I know you don't really promote the bed-and-breakfast this time of year, but whoever it was didn't want to drive back to the Twin Cities tonight if he didn't have to."

"Well, maybe . . ." she said hesitantly. "It *is* the way I cobble together a living—renting out rooms, the Christmas boutique, teaching mornings, and part-time subbing . . ."

"Forget I called. You don't need more on your plate, Merry."

"No, Zeke, wait. Maybe I should. I spent more on stock for the store this year. I need every bit of income I can earn in order to sleep better at night."

"I tell you what, I'll call this guy and tell him that you're normally closed over Christmas but that he can have a room for a hundred and fifty bucks a night, take it or leave it."

"That's highway robbery!"

"Here, maybe, but if he has to drive back to the Twin Cities, a hotel room and gas are going to cost him that. I'll leave the choice to him. I'll call you if he decides to come, okay? It's getting late, but I'll be surprised if he doesn't take you up on it."

"Fine. Let me know."

At that moment a ruckus started in the kitchen.

"Zeke, I've got to go. Peppermint wants out."

"Okay, talk to you soon."

Merry hurried to the kitchen, where her border collie was pacing by the back door. She'd trained Peppy to ring the string of sleigh bells she'd hung on the doorknob when nature called. Unfortunately he enjoyed ringing the bells a little too much, and he'd paw at them until Merry ran into the kitchen to stop him.

After clipping the dog out on his chain, she returned to the house and picked up the phone. The message light was on.

"Hey, Merry, it's Zeke. That guy is coming by. He'll take any room you have and be grateful for it. I checked with my boss. He's a well-respected businessman and apparently has good credentials."

Merry smiled as she put down the phone. Zeke was still watching out for her.

Humming, she heated milk for hot chocolate and put out some peppermint candy cane cookies on a plate for her new guest. She liked her house to be a cozy respite from the harsh realities of the world. Then she hurried upstairs to check the linens and turn on the gas fireplace in the guest room she planned to put him in.

She was descending the stairs when the doorbell rang. She peeked out the lace-covered glass in the door's side window and saw a figure hunched against the cold, his ears buried in his collar.

Merry threw open the door and welcomed him inside. It took a moment to realize who had turned up on her doorstep. Ebenezer Scrooge himself, Jack Frost.

"You!"

He had the grace to look embarrassed. "I'm sure you didn't expect me to return, especially after . . . well, you know . . . that comment about Christmas." He glanced around the room filled floor to ceiling with ornaments, garlands, and gifts. She could sense what he didn't say. He hated it here, the commercialism, the way Frost had changed.

"Now, at least, I know what I'm dealing with. You and I obviously have very different attitudes toward the holiday." She couldn't resist giving him a glance as chilly as the out of doors.

He was treading on dangerous territory when he said anything negative about Christmas. She'd worked hard to create the Christmas she'd yearned for as a child. Making Christmas wonderful for others was the way she combated her own loneliness.

His shoulders sagged as he sighed and ran his fingers through his dark hair.

Merry realized how tired he must be. "Sorry. We'll switch to neutral territory. I've got cocoa and cookies in the kitchen. You can either join me or take them to your room." She turned toward the kitchen door and he followed her.

Without comment, he dropped into one of the chairs and put his head in his hands. "I can't believe every single hotel room was taken."

"We have lives out here in the country too." She set a red-and-green mug in front of him. "High school sports is a big deal for these small communities."

"My mistake. I just assumed . . ." He picked up a cookie and bit the crook off the red-and-white cane.

He was assuming a lot more than just that, Merry thought. Prune down Christmas? He had things to learn about that as well.

Discreetly she watched him down the food in front of him. The tension across his eyes and forehead were obvious, and the tightness in his jaw told her that the day hadn't been an easy one. Well, it hadn't been a picnic for her either, she thought ungraciously.

Shame on me! She quickly readjusted her attitude. How could she judge this complete stranger? Even one whose personality rubbed against hers like a fingernail on a chalkboard.

"Would you like to sign the register?" Merry handed him a record book embossed with the words *Merry's Christmas Boutique and B&B.*

"Merry? Is that how you spell your name? As in Merry Christmas?"

She waved a dismissive hand. "Merry Noel is my mother's idea of a good name for a baby born on Christmas Day."

"I see. Nice. I think."

He followed her up the stairs to the room she had chosen for him. Merry threw open the door to reveal the large room, which at its center had a king-sized four-poster bed dressed with lace and a fluffy down comforter. The firelight flickered in the hearth, leaving the room slightly shrouded in the dimness.

Had she known her guest would be anti-Christmas, she might have moved the mini Christmas tree from the seat in the bay window, but it was too late now. If he didn't like it, he'd have to unplug it.

"Wow," she heard him say as she crossed the floor and turned on a lamp on the antique table she'd found in the attic. "This is amazing."

"Glad you like it. I'm sorry if this room isn't up to your usual standards," she added a little petulantly. She still hadn't quite forgiven him for that crack about Christmas in Frost.

"Listen, I'm sorry about this afternoon. I didn't mean to insult you—or Frost either. It's just that I've chosen to live my life without the trappings of Christmas. They desecrate a holy day. I believe . . ." He broke off and looked up as the fireplace crackled.

Strong words, Merry thought.

"You can turn the fire off from the bed. Here is the remote. There are extra comforters and towels in the cupboard if you need them, and bottled water in the bathroom. Is there anything else I can get you?"

He looked at her ruefully. "I apologize if I offended you. You can blame me for being too blunt."

He yawned sleepily. Somehow he looked much more appealing tonight—a little heavy-eyed, a bit ruffled, and a lot handsome, Merry noted as she backed toward the door. "Good night, Mr. Frost." Merry turned and was gone.

She didn't see him staring after her with a bewildered expression on his features.

"What did you think of him, Peppy?" Merry asked the border collie as she washed her face and readied herself for bed. "You're a good judge of character." The dog had, more than once, reacted with a savvy she sometimes didn't feel herself toward the men she'd dated. Now she only went out with guys Peppy liked.

Peppy whined and put his head on his paws and stared up at her with expressive eyes.

"I notice you didn't even bark at him. Did you like Jack Frost?"

Peppy's tail began to fan softly back and forth across the bathroom floor.

Merry snorted. "That shows me you're losing your touch. You like a man who'd put me out of the Christmas business? Peppy, Peppy, Peppy." She waggled her toothbrush at him. "I'm going to get my take on people from Eggnog from now on."

The cat was a sure bet. He didn't like anyone—especially men.

Chapter Three

Merry awoke to see the sun shining on the pristine blanket of white that had fallen during the night. She arose, shrugged into her robe, and sat down in the recliner she kept by the window. Her prayer chair, she called it. The snow sparkled like diamonds in a jeweler's case, and she marveled at the way it covered the landscape and created a winter wonderland. The woodpile, which had been a dark stain against the snow, was now a perfect white rise in the backyard. The dead tree that needed to come down had become a sculptural vision against the blue sky. Snow hid the defects and washed the world clean, even if only for a little while.

She picked up the Bible from the basket beside her chair and opened it to Isaiah.

"Though your sins are like scarlet, they shall be white as snow; though they are red like crimson, they shall become like wool."

It was why she loved winter. The snow was an ever-present reminder of the forgiveness and cleansing she had in Christ.

The coffee had just finished when she heard footsteps on the stairs.

Mr. Frost entered the kitchen. His dark hair was still damp and his face clean-shaven. Merry felt something like an air tickle in her stomach, the kind she got on the roller coaster at the Minnesota State Fair.

Ignoring that, Merry poured him a mug of coffee and handed it to him. "Good morning."

"Thank you," he said somberly. He took the cup and held it with both hands, warming his palms.

"Chilly? I can turn up the thermostat."

"No, it's just that waking up to snow is a little different for me. I'm psychologically cold, I guess."

"Where's home?" Merry asked as she retrieved cranberry muffins and a fluffy egg bake from the oven.

"California."

"No wonder you're cold. You haven't acclimated yet. Your blood is still thin."

"Is that a medical diagnosis?"

"Not that I know of, but it feels true, doesn't it?" When she returned with the fruit compote, Frost was bowing his head over the table.

Praying. That was encouraging. He believed the Christmas story, no matter what else he thought about the season.

She sat down across from him and passed the egg bake.

"Sorry I'm so casual, but I have to leave too, so I thought we could eat together. I hope you don't mind."

"Not at all. The food is wonderful." He eyed her speculatively. "You could open a restaurant."

"I do occasional meals here," Merry said. "I'm happy to help people with their entertaining." She smiled slightly. "Besides, it pays the bills."

"Is there anything you *don't* do?"

"I'll try anything once. Sometimes it works out better than other times." She hesitated a moment before adding, "Like Christmas. I'm very good at Christmas."

He looked like he was about to say something but then must have changed his mind.

What had she hoped for? A retraction of his disparaging words? With a sigh, she poured juice into his glass and dished up her own food.

"Will you want dinner this evening or do you have plans?" she ventured after some moments of awkward silence.

Frost glanced up, startled. "I won't be back tonight. I plan to get a hotel room in Blue Earth."

"Good luck. The tournament isn't over for a couple more days."

"You're kidding, right?"

"Is it so awful, with the Christmas ornaments and all, that you don't want to spend another night?" she chided gently.

He flushed a little, an attractive warmth coloring his tanned features. It made him seem more human, Merry realized. Until now she'd been disconcerted by his gravity.

"Not at all . . . I don't . . . want to be a nuisance. . . ."

"Have another muffin. They have pecans in them. And don't think for a moment you are a bother. This is part of what I do for a living." Then she blushed herself. "No pressure or anything."

He stared at her, his dark eyes shadowed, unreadable. Then understanding flickered in his gaze. "Of course. Plan on me for tonight. I'll eat in town, however."

Merry felt like kicking herself. She'd meant to sound welcoming, not desperate, but Frost had practically read her mind and deduced the current size of her bank account.

He might be her adversary, she reminded herself. If Frost meant what he said when he arrived, he'd willingly shut her—and Christmas—down entirely.

But Merry didn't have it in her to remain negative very long. By the time Jack Frost had left the house, her mood had brightened again. She hummed as she shoveled the snowy frosting off the sidewalk and driveway and sang along with the radio all the way to work.

"Good morning, I think," Lori Olson greeted her as she walked into the elementary school where they taught together.

"You think? What's going on?"

"I just came from the lunchroom. That new little girl you have in class is down there eating breakfast like it's the first time she's ever tasted food."

Merry's heart sank. Greta Olson was a recent transfer. Merry didn't have the whole story, but it sounded as if the child's family was living week to week between homeless shelters provided by a group of churches. The little girl usually wore the same clothing for two and three days at a time, and her tennis shoes were little protection against the winter weather.

"The child is obviously not being fed properly," Lori said. Disapproval sharpened her tone.

"She has a good appetite, that's all," Merry said non-committally. "She told me she had a grandmother somewhere in the area. Her parents are looking for her."

"Then where is she?" Lori was obviously upset. "And the child is grubby. I don't know what we're going to do about . . ."

"Greta is bathed every day. It's her old clothing that's the problem." Merry held up the bag she was carrying. "Here are new ones. My neighbor has a child Greta's age. I asked her if she had anything her daughter had outgrown. My idea was to keep them here at school and when I could do it discreetly, offer Greta a change of clothing."

Before Lori could say more, Merry added, "The principal is comfortable with this."

The first of the children began to arrive, so Lori and Merry parted. Merry was disturbed. Granted, Greta's clothes were old and worn, but otherwise she was obviously a happy child. And no matter what Lori thought, the child wasn't underfed.

"Miss Blake, look what I brought for show and tell!" A little boy with red hair and a smattering of freckles across his nose pulled a black-mottled, long, leaf-shaped thing from his pocket. "It's my 'speriment."

"*Ex*periment, Danny."

"Yeah, 'speriment." He held the unidentifiable thing up to her face. It smelled faintly moldy. "It's a banana peel. I 'sperimented to see how it would look when it was dry."

Danny was one of her brightest students. Nothing much he did surprised her, but Merry was always impressed with the child's initiative.

Danny's eyes began to sparkle impishly. "And my sister's scared of it. I put it in her bed last night and she really screamed."

"That wasn't very nice, was it, Danny?"

"No, but it was funny!"

Merry was relieved to see the other children begin to arrive. She thought it was funny too, but she didn't dare let Danny know that.

Merry had forgotten about her conversation with Lori until she saw Greta enter the room. She was dressed in pink corduroy pants that were rolled up at the ankles and had worn patches where the knees had been scraped up by their previous owner. Those thin parts now landed on Greta's shins. Her sweatshirt had once belonged to an older boy or else she was a big fan of the trucks displayed across the front. Her pale, flyaway blonde hair circled her head like a halo. That was appropriate, Merry mused, because the child had the face of an angel. Her blue eyes were always wide with wonder, and her smile was quick and ready, despite her circumstances. Greta was as appealing a child as Merry had ever met, and as a kindergarten teacher, she'd met many.

"Do we get to paint today?" Greta asked as she neared. "I love to paint." She clasped her hands together as if to suppress her overwhelming excitement.

"You love to do everything in school, don't you, Greta?"

The child's smile lit her face. "Because it's fun! I like it here better than . . ." Her voice drifted off. Greta frowned, but like light peeking through dark clouds, she smiled again. "I just like it here, that's all."

Though Merry had planned another project for art, that could wait. Today they would paint.

＊ ＊ ＊ ＊ ＊

Abby had opened the doors by the time Merry arrived at the store that afternoon. Two groups of women from the Twin Cities of Minneapolis and St. Paul were already shopping.

"Thanks for opening. I'll try not to be late from now on," Merry said breathlessly as she stowed her coat in the front closet. Abby had lit several candles, and the room was filled with the scent of vanilla and cherries.

Abby eyed her appraisingly, as if she could sense something was amiss, but she held her tongue.

Merry didn't express her concerns about Greta. Instead she pushed those thoughts to the back of her mind for the time being.

"Rebecca from the church stopped by. They've got most of the volunteers for the living Nativity, but they're having a hard time finding a Joseph. The men in town are serving the *lutefisk* dinner at the church that night. They wondered if you might have any ideas."

"I'll come up with someone," Merry said absently as she looked in the till.

"That's what I told them."

Merry didn't respond as one of the shoppers came toward the checkout counter laden with a tangle of garlands.

"Do you have crystal icicles? These would look lovely with icicles dripping from them."

"I have just the thing," Merry assured her and headed to the other side of the room. "Come with me."

And so it went until closing time. As she was about to

lock the door, Mr. Frost appeared on the front step.

Merry waved him in. "Hurry inside. I don't want anyone else to think we're still open." She locked the door,
pulled the shade on the door's window, and flipped the
Open sign to *Closed*.

"Busy day?" He eyed her as if assessing her tousled hair.

She pulled a strand of shiny red garland from around
her neck and dropped it onto the counter.

"At four we had a van load of ladies for a Christmas
tea. I haven't sat down since noon, and all I've had to eat
is gingerbread cookies. If you'd like a snack, come into the
kitchen while I make myself something to eat. Did you have
dinner?" She'd decided on her drive home from school that
she wasn't going to be intimidated by this man, no matter what he said about Christmas or how much of Frost he
owned. From now on, he was simply a guest, not one who
might disrupt everything in this little town she loved.

He shook his head slowly. "I'd planned to, but time got
away from me. I was halfway to Frost before I even remembered I hadn't stopped to eat." He ran his fingers through
the tumble of his dark hair. He looked as though he'd been
doing that a lot. "This has been a frustrating day. Most of
the stuff I'm looking for isn't on a computer, so I'm up to
my ears in dusty old papers." He rubbed the bridge of his
nose with his thumb and forefinger. "And for every step
forward, I seem to be taking two steps back."

Merry felt him trailing behind her as she entered the kitchen. She pointed to a kitchen chair. "Coffee, tea, hot chocolate, eggnog . . .?"

"Coffee, strong."

Something in his voice made her study him. He wasn't as pressed and polished as he'd been this morning. His demeanor was weary. "I'm sorry if you had a bad day."

"I've had better. Also worse. Mostly it was just long. It appears that the deeds on the land my grandfather left have some errors made in recording that need to be corrected."

"Can't that be taken care of?"

"With time. I'd hoped to leave here in a couple days, but that's not possible, I'm afraid. I might as well stick with this now that I'm here."

She put a mug in front of him and a plate of her favorites—white cake bites covered with frosting and crushed peanuts. Then she dropped into the chair across from him. "Does this mean that you'll be staying here awhile longer, or do you plan to find a hotel in Blue Earth?"

He hesitated before answering, she noted.

"I suppose I should get out of your hair during your busy season." He bit into the cake and chewed thoughtfully. "But the food's good here."

She was surprised at the answer, thinking he'd be gone in a heartbeat. "No problem." Merry dipped her head when

she added, "I wouldn't mind the business." *Even from you,
a Christmas Grinch.*

He nodded, deal made. When he was done with his
coffee, he rose from his chair and headed for the stairs. "I
think I'll shower before dinner."

She nodded absently and watched him walk toward the
stairs. His shoulders were broad. He'd probably spent time
lifting weights. His hips were narrow and his legs long.

Merry usually preferred men in blue jeans—casual, laid-
back types who smiled easily and drove pickup trucks—
a result of living in a farming community, most likely. Still,
much to her chagrin, Jack Frost defied all her preferences
and still didn't come up wanting.

The thought didn't linger long, though, as her mind
turned to dinner and to little Greta and her uncertain
future. That was where her prayers needed to focus tonight.

Chapter Four

· · · · · · · · · · · · · · · ·

At 6:00 AM, Merry heard a clattering sound downstairs in the kitchen. No doubt it was Peppy wanting out, or the cat was on the forbidden countertops looking for breakfast. She rolled out of bed, gathered a fleecy pink robe around her, and padded downstairs.

It wasn't Peppy after all, but Jack. Coffee was brewing, Peppy was scarfing down his dog food, and Jack was pouring dry food into Eggnog's dish. The cat was purring loudly and weaving himself around Jack's ankles. It was a very domestic scene.

A glint of surprise shimmered through Merry. Nog was never friendly to strangers, particularly men. Jack was the first male she'd ever seen him cozy up to. In fact, Nog had been known to hiss and plant his claws in the pant leg of more than one erstwhile boyfriend, much to Merry's embarrassment.

In hindsight, however, the cat had been right every time. Nog could spot a loser long before it became apparent to Merry. Maybe the cat was losing his touch, she decided. Nog didn't know the man's attitude toward Christmas!

"I didn't think you'd be up so soon," she said. "I'm sorry I didn't have the coffee ready. We're having omelets for breakfast, so I'll whip one up right now."

"No hurry. I've got an appointment in Blue Earth at ten, but there's plenty of time." He sounded more relaxed than he had last evening, apparently having reconciled himself to being trapped in a small town for a few more days.

Merry hurriedly began to break eggs into a bowl. Thankfully she'd chopped the ham and vegetables last night.

It was disconcerting, however, when Jack took her favorite mug from the back of the sink, filled it with the freshly brewed coffee, and set it on the counter near where she was working. He was serving her coffee? This was all supposed to happen the other way around.

His hair was still damp from the shower, and he was wearing navy trousers and a soft blue shirt rolled up at the sleeves. He looked perfectly at ease in her kitchen, pouring orange juice into glasses and setting the table.

Then Merry caught a glimpse of herself in the glass front of the microwave oven. Her hair was riotous, her eyes still puffy from sleep, and there was a deep crease in her cheek from where she'd lain on her pillow.

"Oh," she squeaked, "oh, oh." She glanced at the cooking eggs. Should she sprint for the bedroom to repair the damage and let the eggs overcook, or make the omelets and be humiliated by the way she looked?

The eggs, she decided. Jack Frost had already seen her looking like a frumpy dowager. Besides, what did it matter?

When the toast was up and buttered, the eggs cooked to perfection, and the grapefruit broiled golden with brown sugar and a maraschino cherry on top, she served the meal.

"I'm going to run upstairs and put on something other than this," she said, indicating her floor-length robe. "Go ahead and eat. I'll be right back."

"It's fine with me. Kind of cozy. I think my mother had a robe like that."

"Thanks, I think, but I think I'll change anyway." She hurried to the stairs wondering what kind of *hausfrau* he thought she was.

Minutes later, clad in comfortable corduroys and one of her more delightfully garish Christmas sweaters, Merry returned to the kitchen. With her hair fixed and her makeup in place, she felt slightly better.

Frost looked up and blinked at her. "That's quite a sweater," he ventured.

"A work of art, don't you think? Imagine how long it took to sew on all these little reindeer." She pointed to Rudolph with his nose so bright. "Do you notice the harnesses are real fake leather?" She fingered the tiny white pom-pom on Santa's hat.

"Real fake leather? Isn't that an oxymoron?"

"Beats me. Want to see the special part?" She pushed on Rudolph's withers, and the reindeer's nose began to glow red. "It works like one of those talking teddy bears—squeeze its paw and it begins to talk. Cute, huh?"

When she heard a strangled sound, she narrowed her eyes and stared at him. He was trying hard not to laugh. "What's wrong?"

"That is the most awful, ugly—*hideous*—sweater I have ever seen!"

She tried and failed to keep the hurt look off her face. "Hideous? This is one of my favorites!"

"*One* of your favorites? You mean there are more?"

"Dozens of them. My friends search rummage and after-Christmas sales for these. They are my uniform both November and December. What's so bad about that?"

"What's so bad is . . ." Then he put his hand to his forehead as if he had a brewing headache. "Maybe we shouldn't get into this right now." He glanced at his watch. "I'd better get going. I have lots to do today." He pushed away from the table, his food half eaten. "Thanks for breakfast."

She watched him go. Hadn't he said only moments before that he had plenty of time? What on earth about her sweater had offended him so? The man *really* didn't like Christmas. Merry glanced around the room. There were Christmas potholders and towels, plates, napkins, and mugs everywhere. There were candles on each windowsill and poinsettias and gingerbread houses on every flat surface. Merry's Christmas Boutique was what she did for a *living*. How could he expect it to look any different? How could he expect *her* to look any different?

Jack Frost had come to town with a grudge against Christmas, bent on somehow banishing it from what she realized she'd begun to refer to in her mind as *his town*. She recalled what she'd read about Jack Frost killing those who aggravated him by covering them with snow. In fact, she felt the flakes piling up right now.

But she wouldn't allow it to bother her. He didn't own her or this house. Let him try to throw a monkey wrench into Frost's Christmas celebration. He'd find a lot of pushback he wasn't expecting—especially from her.

* * * * *

The principal called Merry into the office even before she got to the kindergarten room. Mr. Peterson looked harried, not a good sign so early in the morning. He waved Merry toward a chair. "Lori Olson spoke to me earlier. I need to ask you some questions about Greta. Have you noticed anything in her behavior that might indicate she's been neglected or . . . anything?"

"Other than the fact that she's short of clothing? No. She's a very sweet and happy little girl. I think her parents are just down on their luck."

The principal nodded. "I agree. She's living with her mother and her mother's husband. They've been in a string of shelters. Her mother was very open about it when she registered Greta for school."

"Where's her father?"

"Gone. An accident in the military, somewhere overseas. Since Greta's mother is remarried, she and her daughter don't share the same name. The mother's name is Barker, but Greta's is Olson."

"And there are hundreds of those around," Merry said with a faint smile. In fact, not only was her coworker Lori's name Olson but so was that of her retired neighbor Hildy.

"They are hoping to find the grandmother—her father's mother. Social Services say she used to live in the Twin Cities. Greta's mother suggested that if they could find her, the little girl could stay with the grandmother until she and her husband got their feet back on the ground. Apparently after Greta's father died, Greta's mom went off the deep end for a while and cut off ties with everyone—including her husband's family. She's found her way back, but after she remarried they both lost their jobs. She tried to find Greta's grandmother in Minneapolis but without any luck. "

"They completely lost track of her?"

"The woman moved to somewhere around here, according to old neighbors. That's why the family came to Blue Earth. They thought they could get help if they found her former mother-in-law."

Merry thought of Hildy next door—no, it couldn't be; that would simply be too much of a coincidence. "What is this mystery woman's name?" she ventured anyway.

"Bernice, I think."

That counted Hildy out, Merry mused. Besides, there were tons of Olsons in Minnesota. It would be like finding the proverbial needle in the haystack.

* * * * *

After school Merry saw many cars lined up in front of the shop. Since Abby had opened again today, she probably needed a break.

When she entered the shop, the scents of evergreen and cinnamon assaulted her nostrils. Some of the ladies were shopping, their arms full of stuffed toys or woven throws, and a few were seated in the living room having tea and dainty cookies. Merry had even decorated each and every sugar lump with a bit of red and green to amp up the spirit of the holiday.

Abby was at the till ringing up sales and looked frazzled.

"Welcome! Merry Christmas!" Merry recognized several of the ladies from past years.

"Could you make some of these for me?" One of the women pointed toward the sugar lumps. "They'd be darling on my table." The others cooed in agreement.

"Ah . . . sure. How many?" She really didn't need any more fussing, but special orders were her best moneymakers. She took the orders and headed for the till.

Abby caught Merry's sleeve as she was ringing up the order. "Can I sit down for a couple minutes? My feet are killing me!"

"Absolutely. Has it been busy?"

"They were standing at the front door waiting to get in when I arrived." Abby grinned. "Of course, *everybody* loves Christmas."

Not quite, Merry thought. She was harboring Ebenezer Scrooge right here, right under her own roof.

Ebenezer . . . er . . . Jack arrived for dinner at seven. He looked tired, Merry noted, and worried. Something weighed heavily on him.

She served roasted chicken with mounds of vegetables, creamy white mashed potatoes, and hot rolls. Merry waited until he'd made his way through the first plate and was on to seconds before she asked, "Bad day?"

The weariness in his eyes made them look somber and intense.

She felt a pang of sympathy for him, Scrooge or not.

"For one thing, I've discovered that my great-grandfather

was not the businessman we thought he was. In fact, he was careless and a terrible record keeper. I feel like I'm trying to unravel a skein of tangled yarn."

"So it will take awhile, then?"

"Much longer than I'd planned. Fortunately, this is our slow time of year at my plant. Between Thanksgiving and Christmas we usually see business drop off."

"What do you make?"

"Medical devices. Pacemakers, for example. I have a good staff, which means I can stay here until things are sorted out."

"Things like titles and deeds and who owns what?"

"Exactly. Every single piece of land in town and the rural area has to be sorted through. Houses, cropland, pastures, you name it. I have two first cousins, both women who have small children. Although I inherited this from my father, I want to make sure my cousins and their children get what they need too."

"What do you plan to do with the land—and Frost?" She spooned more mashed potatoes onto her plate and reached for the gravy.

"Sell it all, probably. There's nothing for me here."

"Your family founded this town. The entire town is named after your ancestors, and you don't care in the least?"

"I've been dogged by my name all my life, Merry. I've kept it because someone I loved always called me Jack, but jokes about Jack Frost, references to freezing leaves off the trees, stupid movies that make fun of Jack Frost the buffoon . . . It's all getting old. People enjoy ribbing a real, live Jack Frost. I have to admit I'll be glad to be rid of the town with my name on it."

"Sentimental soul," Merry murmured under her breath. Then she looked up and saw his eyes. "I'm sorry. I shouldn't have said that."

"Apology accepted," he said.

"By the way," Jack said, gracefully changing the subject, "who is Greta? I noticed you prayed for her during grace."

"Greta is a little girl in my class. She and her family are in financial trouble and currently homeless. Greta comes to school in worn-out clothing. She's also a very cheerful, friendly child who doesn't seem to have emotional problems as a result. They are trying to find her grandmother who is supposed to live in this area."

Jack sat back and crossed his arms over his chest. He was silent for a long time before saying, "We so easily get caught up in our own issues that we forget we could have it so much worse." He surprised her by adding, "Is there anything I can do?"

"Unless you can conjure up a grandmother out of thin air or a free house, I don't think so."

Jack didn't say any more, but he looked thoughtful.

Chapter Five

On her way home from school, Merry stopped at the bank to deposit the previous day's checks.

Penny Barlow was at the teller's window. When she saw Merry approach, she waved her over. Penny was what Merry called a professional gossip. Though she was a relatively new resident of Frost, by working where she did, Penny could keep her fingers on the pulses of several small communities in a rural radius of thirty or forty miles. If something happened anywhere in Penny's realm, Merry knew she'd hear about it on her next visit to the bank. Sometimes downloading all her information took Penny a long time. That's why Merry chose to use the drive-up window whenever she could.

"So you have a B-and-B guest at your house." Penny's nose twitched delightedly. "A tall, dark, and handsome stranger too."

"I hadn't thought about it that way, but I suppose you could say that." The conversation made Merry uncomfortable.

"I think he'll be there for a while," Penny whispered. "Good luck, because I don't think he's happy about it."

Merry thought back to Jack's reference to the state of his family affairs. "Should you be telling me this?"

Penny waved a hand dismissively. "Oh, it's not about bank business. My friend at the Register of Deeds office in Blue Earth said—"

"Don't tell me. She's not supposed to be talking about Mr. Frost's business either." It was the one thing about small-town life that Merry had never quite grown accustomed to. Everyone knew everyone else's business. Sometimes it seemed that others knew her business *before* she herself did. In Minneapolis people sometimes didn't know their own neighbors. Here, only a hundred miles away, it was a completely different story. Still, she didn't regret opening her Christmas store in a town so aptly named. It was as if it were meant to be. She'd been hired for her teaching job the same week she'd decided to make the move.

"And that's another thing! Isn't it crazy? *Jack Frost!* In Frost. Now, right before Christmas!" Penny's brow furrowed. "He's gorgeous, of course, but kind of grumpy according to my friend. He doesn't seem to like his relatives very much. Or Christmas either. I thought a guy with a name like that would be crazy about the season. He made some disparaging remark about Frost turning into a Christmas carnival. He's like the Grinch!"

Merry managed to excuse herself before Penny could reveal more unwelcome gossip and escaped into the street.

A cloud of gloom descended upon her as she drove the nine and a half miles toward Frost. Jack and little Greta Olson were two complications she hadn't planned on.

Greta was such a sweet, happy child despite her family's current circumstances. Joy in the face of discouragement—that was Greta. And Jack . . . he was the picture of discouragement about what she would have thought of as a blessing. He didn't seem to want what had fallen into his lap—the quaint little town she loved. Both people, for very different reasons, pulled at her heartstrings.

When she pulled into her driveway at one o'clock, she noticed Hildy Olson next door struggling to put up a Christmas wreath on her front door. Hildy was a tall woman with short, iron-gray hair and a determined expression. She'd been a few pounds overweight when Merry first met her, but those pounds had fallen off over the past few months, and now her jacket fell loose around her.

Hildy never asked for help. Ever. With steely resolve she tackled every project herself. Sighing, Merry walked across the yard to where Hildy was struggling with the wreath.

"Don't say a word," Merry warned her cheerfully. "Let me put that thing up."

"I don't need help," Hildy muttered. "If I could just get the thingamabob in the gizmo . . ."

Merry took it out of Hildy's hands, and with experience born of much practice, she hung and fastened the wreath, fluffed out the bow, and turned on the battery-operated twinkle lights woven into the greens. "There."

"I could have gotten it . . . eventually," Hildy admitted ruefully.

"But you did the right thing letting me, a self-proclaimed Christmas decorating expert, do it in a couple minutes." Merry put her hand on Hildy's arm. "Now you can come to my house and have a cup of tea instead of wasting your time out here. One day I'll come over and help you string the lights on your porch."

"I'm not doing it this year. This wreath is it. Now I'm done with Christmas."

Shades of Jack Frost!

"Not you too!"

Hildy looked at her. "What?"

"Oh, never mind. Just come over." Merry tugged encouragingly on the older woman's sleeve. "I want to hear what turned you into Ebenezer Scrooge."

Hildy snorted. "That's a long story I won't get into, but I will have some of your peppermint tea."

"Good. Come with me." This, at least, was a start.

Merry put on the teakettle and dished out a plate of her buttery spritz cookies while the water was heating. Then she sat down across from her neighbor at the kitchen table. "Tell me what's wrong."

"Nothing I want to get into, Merry," the older woman

said gently. "It brings up sad memories. I just don't feel like Christmas this year."

"It's the birth of Christ."

"Well, there is that. I'll go to church, of course, but none of this whiz-bang fancy stuff. Christ is all I need for Christmas."

"He's all any of us need," Merry agreed, "but I like to think of this as His birthday party. I serve birthday cake every day in December, and when people ask me why, I can tell them about Him. It's a gentle way to remind people what the season is really about."

"Good for you. Just count me out this year."

There was nothing more to get out of Hildy, Merry knew. She was a woman who kept her own counsel and would only tell Merry what was troubling her when she was good and ready. Merry had no doubt, however, that it would come out eventually.

* * * * *

The windows rattled and the house shook when Jack plowed through the front door and slammed it behind him. Bells on a string jingled and the Clap On, Clap Off light went dark. Several shoppers who were sniffing candles in order to decide which fragrance to buy looked up, startled.

Merry put her finger to her lips to indicate that he should be more circumspect, but she was met with a black glare that could have sliced metal.

"Come into the kitchen," she said. "You look like an angry old bear. I've got beef stew cooking. Maybe a full stomach will help."

Jack looked chagrined and followed her.

With swift hands, she dished up a bowl of stew from the Crock-Pot, thrust a spoon in the bowl, and broke off a hunk of French bread. "Eat. I'll go ring up these last sales and be back. Don't break anything while I'm gone."

When she returned a few minutes later, Jack was serving himself a second bowl of stew and had taken the butter out of the refrigerator for his bread. He'd calmed down, but the look on his face bordered on bleak.

Quietly, she filled a bowl for herself and cut two huge slices of fresh chocolate cake and put them on the table. She sat down, bowed her head for a silent prayer, and began to eat.

"I'm sorry about how I came in," Jack said contritely. His remarkable eyes looked genuinely repentant.

Merry hadn't noticed before how long and dark his eyelashes were. Nor had she noticed that his profile was nearly flawless.

"It's just that I've never had such an exasperating day in my life. I had no right to storm in here like that. I forgot you might have customers."

Since you'd never buy any of the things I sell, you assume no one will? she thought but left unspoken.

"Frankly," he said, half to himself, "I don't know how my ancestors succeeded at anything with their lack of organization. My great-grandfather allowed buddies of his to farm his land when he was alive. It was all in a letter he wrote to someone at the courthouse. Although he never sold the land and no money ever changed hands, that left the next generations to assume the property belonged to them. Since none of the land has ever changed hands and the taxes have been paid annually out of an interest-bearing account set up years ago, now I'm in the uncomfortable position of telling families that they don't own the land they live on and never have.

"No one ever questioned why the taxes were paid directly from that account. I think every party assumed it was *their* great-grandfather who'd set it up."

"And if it's not broken, don't fix it?"

"Right. But the result is that I have no idea how much property was 'loaned' to people and forgotten about."

"Oh dear," Merry blurted. "How awful for you! You mean you'll have to kick people out of their homes?"

Jack looked at her miserably.

"Can't you just let them stay?" Even as she said it she knew it was a ridiculous idea. Jack's family owned the property. He had every right to his own inheritance.

"I'm afraid I'll be the most despised man in Frost before I'm done, but it can't be any other way. These people have to buy me out, move, or start farming for me and paying rent. I can't just turn the land over to them . . . there are my cousins to consider."

They sat silently, both looking down at the table and the cooling stew. Merry wasn't hungry anymore. This was an awful situation for Jack and for the yet unknowing people who had assumed for years his land was theirs.

"So this might take awhile to untangle?" she finally ventured. "And you'll need a place to stay?"

He looked at her and gave a humorless smile—the only kind he seemed to have. "Two or three weeks, I'm afraid."

"Won't you have to go back to your company?"

"I've got good people, and I check in every day. Unless something unforeseen happens, it will be business as usual there. I just never expected anything like this or planned on spending so long in Frost. Especially now."

He didn't elaborate further, but Merry had a good idea what he'd meant—especially now during the holiday season, with this little place on Christmas steroids. It was going to be a very long few weeks.

She poured the coffee and suggested, "Maybe a distraction would be good. I own lots of Christmas movies. Want to watch one?"

"What are my choices?" His eyes narrowed suspiciously.

She ticked them off on her fingers. "*The Christmas Carol, Polar Express, Home Alone, Miracle on 34th Street . . .*" She saw his expression and added, " . . . movies that you would probably find annoying."

"I'm sorry I don't hold your view of Christmas superficiality. There are reasons, Merry, but I don't want to go into that." His features showed unspoken pain. "Let's just say it's simply too frivolous for my taste."

Merry felt a rush of frustration churn through her. "Jack, I would never do anything that sullied this holiday! But it is a birthday, the birthday of the King of kings! No one leaves my business without knowing that's what I believe. It's an opportunity to share with others what Christmas is truly about. It's my witness."

His expression softened. "I realize that."

"What *do* you believe about Christmas, Jack?"

He stared over her shoulder and out the window, where the winter darkness was total. A bright moon backlit the leafless trees that bordered her yard.

"It's a long story, Merry. We should save it for another time."

There was firmness in his voice that brooked no argument. There wouldn't be another time, Merry realized. He didn't want to talk about it, so he *wouldn't* talk about it.

Pasting her best hostess smile on her face, she said, "Of course. It's really none of my business anyway. More coffee?"

Chapter Six

Jack watched her make her way around the kitchen in her fluffy slippers. The woman's entire wardrobe seemed to consist of things that were soft, fuzzy, fluffy, red, or green. She was an unlikely looking businesswoman who was perfect for her job. He'd never run into anyone quite like her . . . fortunately. This much Christmas spirit was going to bring him to his knees.

Still, to be fair, she didn't know why Christmas was such a difficult time of year for him. He'd been accused by many women of being somber, aloof, and inscrutable. Ironically that usually made them more interested in him, until they discovered there was no way beneath the tough shell he wore. He cultivated that armor for a reason. It kept him from remembering the day his entire family fell apart.

He didn't realize the dog was under the kitchen table until Peppy uncurled himself and thrust his nose from beneath the tablecloth, interrupting Jack's musings. Peppy stretched, paws forward, and yawned so widely he displayed an entire mouthful of white teeth and pink gums and tongue. If Jack looked fully into that mouth, he'd probably see the inside of the tip of Peppy's tail.

The dog then sauntered to the back door and bumped his nose on a string of silver bells Jack hadn't noticed until now. Merry automatically opened the door and Peppy raced outside.

"What's that about?"

"The bells, you mean? I get involved in things around the store and forget to take poor Peppy out, so I taught him to ring the sleigh bells when he needs to go outside. We're both happier as a result."

He wanted to accuse her of kidding him, but it was obviously true. She had the dog ringing sleigh bells all year long, he'd guess, summer included.

As if she'd read his mind, she said, "I love hearing sleigh bells in the summer."

"You are an incorrigible Christmas addict."

Merry's smile brightened. "I am, aren't I? Thank you!"

He hadn't meant it to be a compliment, just an observation, but Merry looked as if he'd handed her an armful of roses.

Mentally, he surrendered. He'd never understand this woman. Fortunately he didn't have to. As soon as he'd straightened out this mess his long-dead relative had made, he could go back to California, where the sun always shone and it was much, much easier to ignore the trappings of Christmas.

"Maybe I'll just go upstairs," Jack said as he pushed away from the table. "I have some reading to do, and I should check in with my business team. I can't make myself too dispensable or they'll never notice I'm missing." He smiled ruefully.

"You have a nice smile," Merry blurted. "You should do it more often." She blushed. "Sorry, I've got a big mouth. Or at least one that refuses to stay shut. I didn't mean to sound so personal. No offense?"

"None taken." He'd found it was hard not to smile around this woman, even though those muscles were rarely exercised these days. He hadn't felt like smiling this much for a very long time.

Abruptly he pushed away from the table, thanked her for the food, and retreated to his room, where he paced until he had his thoughts under control.

It was a pleasant spot, he considered, with a comfortable reading chair, an antique table that acted as a desk, and the fireplace that felt wonderful on these cold nights. It even had Wi-Fi and cable television. And great food. He really couldn't ask for more.

The phone rang. "Frost here."

"Yo, boss, what's up?"

"Hi, Vince. Shouldn't I be asking you that question?"

"We're great here. Don't even know you're gone."

"That's not exactly comforting." Vince had been with him for ten years and could practically read his mind. He also knew more about Jack's past than any other person on the planet.

"But there are things that crop up . . ."

"Thank goodness."

"We need somebody to sign purchase orders, for one thing. You know how fussy accounting is if they haven't gone through you."

"They should be. I threatened them with something dire if one ever got past them."

"I'll overnight them to you. How can I expect to get them back? Pony Express?"

"I have Wi-Fi. I'll scan them once they're signed and send them to accounting. I'll even call and tell them they're coming so they get off your back."

"Wi-Fi? What's next in Podunk, USA? A movie theater with talking pictures? Fast food? ATMs?"

"You're a California snob, Vince. It would do you good to come to the Midwest. It has a lot going for it that you don't know about."

"That vast open space between LA and New York? No thanks. You can tell me about it though. How's the place you finally found to stay?"

"Good. Some parts are great and others . . ."

"And others?" Vince encouraged.

"The little town of my youth has been hijacked by Christmas frivolity."

Vince whistled. "I'll bet you love that. How did that happen? I thought Frost had less than two hundred people."

"Apparently it takes just one to change that." Jack told him about Merry's Christmas Boutique, the tea parties, the bed-and-breakfast, and even the sleigh-bell-ringing dog.

"There are elves in the trees, decorations that would put Martha Stewart to shame, and women baking cookies in the church kitchen day and night. And for some reason unbeknownst to me, they're planning a lutefisk dinner for the entire town."

"What's lutefisk?" Vince asked.

"Fish." Jack decided not to explain further. Vince needed to experience that for himself.

"I don't see anything wrong with that. But I do understand that you might be upset about the other stuff. You can't let it get to you. Life goes on, Jack."

"I know, I know. And mine should go on too. Well, it has. My business is booming, I have friends. . . ." Jack started to pace back and forth across the room, from the entry to the bay windows and back again, suddenly restless.

"That's not what I meant and you know it."

"Let's not talk about this anymore," Jack said, trying very hard not to sound like he was pleading. He hated it when Vince went down this path.

"Then tell me more about this Santa fiasco you're embroiled in."

"Everyone in town is gung ho about celebrating Christmas—a holiday ice fishing tournament, the Parade of Lights that apparently boils down to tractors and old cars strung with lights driving down Main Street, and there's a partridge in every pear tree." Jack took another turn around the room.

"This silly woman Merry Blake has turned the town into a mini Las Vegas of Christmas lights, gifts, and kitschy decorations!"

He realized at once that he'd raised his voice loud enough that it could be heard plainly in the hallway. Hopefully Merry was nowhere around. Then he heard Peppy's sleigh bells ring in the kitchen and Merry's footsteps just outside his door. They passed by and the stairs creaked as she went to let the dog outside.

She must have been at the hallway closet where the bedding, towels, shampoo, and other sundries were kept. Now he could only hope he hadn't been overheard.

"Gotta go, Vince. Call you tomorrow." He went to the door, ready to apologize. Then he thought better of it. Maybe she hadn't heard him. He hoped desperately that she hadn't. She was a sweet woman. The last thing she needed was her guest bad-mouthing her dream, no matter how strongly he disagreed with it.

* * * * *

A silly woman who had turned the town into a mini Las Vegas of Christmas lights, gifts, and kitschy decorations, huh? Is that what she was? Merry tried her hardest not to stomp down the stairs to the kitchen. Peppy was lying on the floor by the door, looking innocent and in no hurry to get out. He rose slowly as she entered.

"Peppy, were you just playing again? Every time you want me you can't be ringing that bell! Only when you need to go out, okay?"

The dog's eyes were bright and intelligent, and he seemed to nod in agreement. Of course, that was in her imagination, and she knew very well that he'd do it again—and again. It was a game he played. Merry knew that she'd have to be the one to learn to discern between nature's call and Peppy's desire for human companionship.

Merry sat down on a chair and buried her nose in the fur at the ruff of the dog's neck. "Oh, Peppy, I just heard what Jack Frost really thinks of me." It might have been better if she'd never heard, but it was done now and she had to decide what to do about it.

At the moment, she was very tempted to "un-invite" Jack from her house. Then the same verse in the first book of Peter that so often inspired her now began to chastise her.

"Show hospitality to one another without grumbling."

God was big on hospitality.

"Lord, help me with this!" she petitioned anxiously. "How am I supposed to be hospitable to someone I'd like to punch in the eye?"

After a little conversation with God, Merry had calmed down enough to coax both Peppy and Nog up to her bedroom. She put on her softest pajamas, gathered her hair into a bundle that resembled a spouting whale, and secured the hair bundle with a band. Then she walked to her bookshelf and pulled out one of the old photo albums from her childhood.

Her mother had been diligent about recording every moment of her only child's life. Pictures were neatly ordered, giving a linear perspective of young Merry Noel's existence. Days after her birth . . . learning to eat solid food and dispensing most of it on the top of her head . . . standing beside a Christmas tree decorated with red bows—it was all there. There was a photo of Christmas every year—only one. Sometimes Merry held a birthday cake as she stood there, giving a nod to the fact that Christmas was also her birthday.

The only whimsical thing her parents had ever done, she'd decided long ago, was to name their daughter Merry Noel.

The memories of her first years were good. Her parents always put forth the effort to make Christmas extra special.

Sometimes there would be two birthday cakes—one for her and one for baby Jesus. It wasn't until she was five or six that she began to realize that Christmas was celebrated very differently at the houses of her friends.

Families came together. Cousins frolicked. Aunts and uncles chatted. Grandmothers cooked and served meals, and great grandmothers smiled benevolently from their rocking chairs. Or, at least that was how Merry imagined it to be. Christmas was for families, a time to come together and celebrate the birth of the Lord.

Each year her own Christmas, celebrated with only her mother and father, seemed smaller and lonelier. They tried hard to make it a special day, but Merry longed to be a part of one of those large families. As much as she loved her parents and all they did for her, Christmas came to connote two very different things in her young mind—the glorious birth of a Savior . . . and loneliness.

When she was fourteen, Merry decided to do something about it. She would bring Christmas to others. Or she would bring others to Christmas. Suddenly Christmases at their home were changed. Merry acted like an undercover spy for six weeks before December 25. If she heard of anyone who didn't have a place to go for dinner, she told her mother, who dutifully invited the individual, often someone she didn't even know, to their home.

As the parties grew, so did Merry's joy. At seventeen,

she made up her mind—she would do everything in her power to make sure everyone had a family for Christmas.

That had led, in a roundabout way, to the store. She'd volunteered to set up a Christmas shopping event for families of children who came to the local food shelf with their parents. Each child could "spend" a penny, a nickel, or a quarter—whatever they had—on a gift for each parent. Businesses began donating gifts, and the event turned into a huge party.

That success as a teenager ultimately emboldened her to open a small Christmas store in Frost. And the rest was history.

She wouldn't let Jack's hurtful comments stop her. He thought she was crazy. She thought he was an iceman emotionally.

Who knew? Merry thought. Maybe she was the one meant to thaw his frozen heart.

Chapter Seven
....

Breakfast was destined to be a quiet affair. Even Peppy knew enough not to start ringing the bells at the back door.

Jack trudged into the kitchen wearing a wary expression, as if he were afraid a frying pan or an airborne egg strata might come flying his way.

Merry, however, kept her back to him, turning only briefly to plop a bowl of homemade granola and a toasted bagel slathered with butter in front of him. She'd filled a carafe with coffee so she wouldn't have to serve it and made sure cream cheese, honey, and jam were already on the table.

She wasn't angry, just hurt. She tried so hard to make her home and store a joyous place, but, ironically, she'd failed miserably with Jack Frost. Surely someone with that name should be pro-Christmas!

Finally Merry had to turn toward the table with a platter of hickory-smoked bacon. When she placed the plate in front of Frost, his fingers closed around her wrist.

"So you heard me talking on the phone?"

"I didn't intentionally eavesdrop. I was putting away towels and . . ."

"I'm sure you weren't. It's me that owes you an apology. I was out of line. I was talking to Vince, my best friend. I was tired and it made me stupid. You aren't silly, and the store isn't kitschy. Vince would tell you I have a problem with Christmas. What I said says more about me than it does about you. I hope you'll accept my apology."

She could almost physically feel his regret. Jack wasn't a bad guy. He was just, in her opinion, really messed up about Christmas. He seemed to have faith—he prayed willingly and comfortably at meals and had a solemn respect for the holiday but complete intolerance for anyone else's vision.

Merry knew what she had to do: show him grace. She'd received enough of that herself to know she was not the one to withhold it from others.

"It's okay. I *am* silly sometimes, and everyone has a right to their own opinion about what I do."

"No one has a right to belittle another human being. It wasn't even about you, not really. Any attitudes I have about this season are mine and mine alone."

She dropped into the chair next to him. He was still holding her wrist, but it was a very gentle touch and she didn't mind. In fact, to her surprise, she rather liked it. "Apology accepted."

She was surprised when his shoulders drooped with relief. So he didn't have an impenetrable fortress built around his heart. Though a rich, successful, and handsome man, he had his share of issues as well.

Merry found herself liking him better. He was very, very human, just like her.

After that, breakfast was a relaxed affair until Merry glanced at the clock. "I'd better get going or I'll be late." She began to shrug into her winter coat and tucked her feet into her boots. "Relax. Take your time. There's more coffee."

She wrapped a lengthy red scarf around her neck and grabbed her canvas bag. "See you tonight?"

"Yes. If you're sure, that is . . ."

"Ancient history. Have a good day." Merry scratched Peppy's head and closed the door behind her.

Whistling softly, she buckled herself into the driver's seat of her car and turned the key in the ignition. Nothing.

She tried again, paying more attention this time. Still nothing. Frowning, she glanced around the interior and her gaze settled on the passenger door. It was ajar. Her battery was dead.

Merry raced back into the house at twice the speed she'd left it. Jack was still at the kitchen table drinking coffee and scratching behind Peppy's ear. The dog appeared hypnotized as he rested his chin on Jack's leg. More surprising was the fact that the cat was sleeping in the sun at Jack's feet.

"What's wrong?" Jack straightened in his chair, and Peppy gave Merry a disgusted look.

"I left my car door open last night. I was carrying groceries in and must not have closed it fully. I'm supposed to be at school in twenty minutes!"

"I'll drive you. Then I'll come back and get your battery charged. Let me know what time you want to be picked up after school."

"You can't do that!"

"Why not? I know how to drive." He sounded amused.

"You've got work to do. You shouldn't have to bother with me."

Jack put his hands on Merry's shoulders to stop her from spinning around the room like a top. "I'll drive you," he pronounced each word slowly, as if speaking to an upset child. "Please. I'd like to help you. I'd feel better if you'd let me."

Merry grew still. That, she understood. "Well, if *you'd* feel better . . ."

"I'll get my jacket and my keys."

* * * * *

Merry squirmed in her seat all the way to Blue Earth. "I'll have a tow truck come out and jump the car. There's no use having you bother with it."

"No bother. Don't spend the money."

That seemed to register with her. Money, he'd realized, was fairly limited in Merry's world. It never had been in his.

"But how . . ."

"Don't worry. I was a teenage boy once. I know a lot about cars. I took a few apart and put them back together in my day."

She looked thoughtful, as if she were trying to imagine it. It struck Jack how attractive she was. He'd been turned inward so long that it really hadn't fully registered earlier. Her features were delicate, her skin porcelain, like peaches-and-cream. There was a fragility about her that was easy to forget because of her outgoing personality. The sunlight filtered through her pale golden hair, and it haloed around her head. She chewed on her rosy lower lip. Jack found it very endearing.

"It still seems like a lot to ask."

He pulled up to the sidewalk near the school. He'd gotten to know the town very well in the past few days. As Merry was about to swing her legs out of the car, a little girl with golden curls and remarkable blue eyes came dashing toward them.

"Miss Blake, Miss Blake!"

The child was a study in contrasts, Jack realized. Her face was truly lovely, the kind of child one sees on television commercials and print ads, but her clothing looked as though it had been worn too many times and by too many children. And her eyes were filled with tears.

"What's wrong, sweetie?" Merry asked when the little girl nearly crumpled into her lap.

"My mommy and daddy are in trouble 'cause we don't have a house to live in." Pools of tears welled in the child's blue eyes and began to leak down her cheeks. "I want to be with my mommy and daddy!"

"Who says you can't?" Merry's voice was clipped and angry.

"Miss Lori. She told another teacher I wasn't being taken care of, but I am. My mommy takes good care of me!"

Merry shot Jack a pleading glance.

He shrugged helplessly. What was he supposed to do?

"I'll walk you inside, Greta. I'd like to speak with Miss Lori myself." Merry turned to Jack. "Thank you so much for the ride."

"What time shall I pick you up?"

"I'll try to get a ride home, thanks."

"No problem. I'll bring your vehicle. It will need to run for a while anyway."

Distracted, Merry sighed. "My kindergarten class is over at lunchtime. Twelve thirty would work."

"See you then."

Jack drove off before Merry could protest. Something in that little girl's eyes nearly broke his heart. Fear and confusion marred that innocent face, things that should be far removed from the life of a five-year-old child.

* * * * *

Greta was unusually quiet this morning. Even Danny, who'd brought his pet hamster, Puffy, for show and tell, couldn't draw the little girl out of her somber mood.

Troubled, Merry went to the teachers' lounge in search of Lori Olson at recess.

Three teachers were seated at the long lunchroom table that constituted their break area. Lori was relating her thoughts about Greta's home situation to the others who listened raptly. "Poor little thing. Have you seen the getup she has on today? Her jeans are so long the folded cuffs are a half-inch thick. Everything she wears is either too big or too small!"

"Sometimes that happens when you shop rummage sales, Lori. The fashion designers have a day off." Merry's voice was soft but steady.

Lori spun around and a flush spread up her neck and across her cheeks. "Merry! I didn't hear you come in. We were just talking about . . ."

"I heard what you were talking about, Lori, but I'm not sure your opinions about Greta's welfare are well-founded."

"Her clothes . . ."

"Are always clean," Merry said firmly. "Just old. That doesn't mean she isn't well cared for. It does indicate that the family is being frugal."

Silently the other two teachers stood up, tossed their coffee cups in the trash, and slipped out of the room, apparently unwilling to witness the confrontation.

"What is it with you and this little girl, Merry? You keep saying you think her home life is okay. It's obvious by the way Greta's dressed that it's not!"

"There's more to parenting than clothes. Greta is cheerful, happy, engaged, and bright. She shows a lot of potential. She's untroubled by her family's situation"—Merry gave Lori a hard look—"as long as others stay out of it."

"What's that supposed to mean?" Lori's eyes narrowed.

Merry wasn't eager to say more, but she didn't like Lori's openly verbal opinions floating around the school.

"Greta is upset today."

"I told you so . . ." Lori looked smug, as if she had seen something others hadn't.

"About the things she heard you saying."

That made Lori pause. "Me?"

"She overhead you tell another teacher that her parents weren't taking care of her. She told me you said that her parents will be in trouble because they don't have a house to live in. Now she's afraid she will be taken away from her family. Lori, that's unacceptable behavior! Talking about one of the children so that they overhear it? You don't know what's going on in that family, nor do I. I've discussed it with the administration, who have talked to Greta's mother. They don't see any need for immediate concern."

"I certainly didn't mean for her to hear what I said." Lori had the grace to look ashamed. "I'm sorry, Merry. It's just that when I think a child might be being mistreated . . ."

"That child is in my class, and I think she's anything but mistreated. Her family is poor, not cruel!"

Lori stared at Merry. "I've never seen you like this before."

"I've never been this angry, that's why. That little girl doesn't need to think she'll be taken from her parents! I'd love to find that grandmother of Greta's. That would solve a lot of issues for everyone."

"But no one knows who she is!"

Merry couldn't debate that. She'd been in the white pages online looking for a Bernice Olson in Minnesota. None lived in this immediate area. But this was the season of miracles, Merry told herself. Then she looked at Lori's crestfallen face.

"Sorry if I came down on you too hard," Merry murmured. "When Greta told me what happened, I lost it."

"I deserved it," Lori admitted. She made a zippering movement across her mouth. "No more speculating, especially not where children might overhear."

"Thank you." Merry turned and left the break room. She hoped Lori wouldn't be upset with her, but she'd said what she needed to say. She felt like a mother lion protecting her cub where Greta was concerned.

* * * * *

Jack drew up to the school in Merry's car and watched kindergarten children pour out of the doors. It was some time before he spotted Merry. She was holding a child's hand as they walked toward a tall young woman with shiny dark hair. The little boy released Merry's hand and ran into his mother's open arms. He spun out of them after a brief hug and reached again for Merry. The adults laughed and Merry put the child back into his mother's embrace.

Then another parent came up to her. And another. Merry was the most popular girl on the playground, Jack mused. Finally she made it to the car.

"I wasn't sure you'd ever get here," Jack commented as she slid into the vehicle. "What are you? Most Admired Teacher of the Year?"

Her laughter was like music in his ears.

"I see you got my car running," she commented, deflecting the attention from herself.

"Yes. I thought I'd better drive it a little. I hope you don't mind."

....

"Mind? I feel like a princess! Usually I'm alone with my car troubles. This is great!"

Somehow that little phrase "usually I'm alone" struck a chord in him. Though he tried to ignore it, he, too, felt alone far too often.

When they arrived in Frost, a black Volvo was parked in Merry's driveway. Merry jumped out of the car and hurried up the garage stairs, leaving Jack to follow.

Inside, a good-looking blond fellow in a business suit was sitting at the kitchen table reading the *St. Paul Pioneer Press*, drinking coffee, and looking as comfortable as if he did it every day of the week.

Jack immediately felt a stab of resentment. Who was this guy making himself at home in Merry's house?

Someone she knew very well, he realized when Merry raced across the room, gave the fellow a quick hug, and shone a smile on him.

"Zeke, what are you doing here in the middle of the day?"

"I drove out to see how you were doing." He tipped his head toward Jack, who still loomed in the doorway.

Merry waved Jack over. "Zeke, this is Jack Frost. Jack, Zeke is the one who lined you up to stay at my B-and-B."

Jack stretched out his hand. "Pleased to meet you. I have you to thank for a roof over my head—and great cooking, I might add."

Zeke nodded knowingly. "The best. Glad it's working out." He turned back to Merry. "How are things in the store?"

"My hard work is finally beginning to pay off. I've had more customers from the Twin Cities and surrounding communities than ever before. Christmas has been good for Frost."

An empty feeling grew in the pit of Jack's belly as he sat down on a chair on the far side of the table. His long-dead relatives now had him embroiled in this holiday funfest, something he'd avoided all his adult life. The emptiness grew into an aching pain in his gut. Maybe this was what he got for suppressing all his negative feelings and emotions over the years. Everything that reminded him of his past was flying in his face, taunting him. Perhaps his father had been right, that ignoring a problem didn't make it go away. It just made it harder to deal with when the time came—and it was inevitable that he'd have to deal with it sooner or later.

He watched Merry interact with Zeke and felt a twinge of jealousy. She laughed easily with him and was no longer on guard. There was something special between them— if not now, there had been—and the fondness for each other hadn't faded.

Jack recognized it even though he'd always done everything in his power to avoid that sort of intimacy. The last thing he'd wanted was a woman to somehow get beneath the shell he'd built to protect himself and force him to share the things he'd suppressed for so long.

They probably didn't want him there, sitting like a lump of coal in a kitchen chair, listening to what they were saying. Maybe they had things to discuss—private things. He rose and cleared his throat. "I think I'll go upstairs. Nice to meet you, Zeke." He left quickly, not wanting to exchange any more small talk with Merry and her boyfriend.

As Jack walked out of the room, Zeke lowered his voice. "He's as icy and reserved as you said, Merry. His name is very fitting. Now how about some of those almond cookies you made for me?"

Jack felt the color drain from his face as he mounted the stairs to his room. What did it matter what Merry or anyone else thought of him? He'd never bothered to care before. Then he realized that he truly didn't care what Zeke What's-His-Name thought of him. It was Merry's opinion that had begun to matter.

How on earth had he let that happen?

* * * * *

The next day, as she was closing the boutique, Hildy arrived on Merry's doorstep with a steaming pot swathed in dishtowels.

"What's this?" Merry asked as she beckoned the older woman inside.

"Chicken and dumplings. I thought you could use help with supper. I saw how many cars were parked outside today. You must be exhausted."

"Bless you, Hildy. I am tired. Not having to cook sounds great, but I'll only accept if you'll join us."

"You've got that man staying here, don't you?"

"Yes. I'd like to have you meet him. You lived in Frost in years past. Maybe you can help him answer some of his questions."

"I moved away when I was a young woman and didn't come back until last year. I can't imagine how I'd do him any good."

"No matter, you'll do me some good."

"My guest, Mr. Frost, has inherited some land in this area," Merry said as she and Hildy set the table and tossed a salad.

"So I've heard," Hildy responded enigmatically. The woman's features were stoic.

"Not all good things, apparently."

"You know how gossip travels. It's never right by the time it gets to the likes of me. People don't like the idea, though, of someone else owning so much of their hometown."

"I'm not sure he likes it either, but he's got to get things sorted out. He can't leave it for another generation!"

Hildy nodded. "I guess there are a lot of things we don't like in this life, but we get used to them."

At that moment, Merry heard Jack's footsteps on the stairs. He must have smelled the delicious aromas coming from the kitchen.

"Just in time," she greeted him. "My neighbor Hildy brought the food."

Her breath, she noticed, was coming faster when Jack neared, and her heart raced. Even Zeke had never affected her quite like that. He smiled at her, and she felt a little hitch in her chest. He reached for her hand and, as if it had its own will, it took his.

They walked together into the dining room and, introductions made, the threesome sat down at the table.

"Hildy, would you like to say grace?" Merry requested.

The woman bowed her head and took a deep breath. "Lord, we don't know how You work. All we can do is trust that Your timing is right, Your love is true, and Your grace plentiful. Whatever pain is on the hearts of each of us tonight, we ask You to intervene and turn it into blessing. Thank You for the food, the fellowship, and the bright joy of Christmas. Amen."

Hildy had a way of reaching into one's heart with her prayers, Merry noted. She must have reached deep into Jack's tonight. He had lost the color in his face, and he stared at Hildy as if she'd just revealed something very personal about him to the world. Then he gathered himself together and turned to his food. He ate with his head down, eyes fixed on his plate.

It was some moments before he looked at her again. There was an expression on his face that Merry couldn't define. Pain? Regret? Or maybe her imagination was working overtime. Perhaps it was just plain gratitude that they had a new cook for the night.

"I don't know how to repay Merry or you, Hildy, for the amazing food I've had while I'm here," Jack pronounced after dinner. He pushed away from the table and leaned back so only the two back legs of the chair rested on the floor. He was relaxed again after whatever had been troubling him.

Hildy snorted. "You're paying your bill, aren't you? As for me, I enjoy cooking for more than one. My husband and son could practically eat us out of house and home. Now, if I cook a roast, I'm eating it in sandwiches, hash, and steak salads for a week." She eyed Jack. "Maybe next week I'll bring one over. Will you still be here?"

"I hope not, but the way things are going it's likely. I'll probably be here until January."

"What about Christmas?" Merry interjected. "Don't you have plans for Christmas?"

Jack shrugged. "Not really. I usually go to church on Christmas Eve and to Vince's place for pizza on the twenty-fifth."

"That's it?" Merry looked aghast.

"I don't plan even that, but it's usually how it works out. Otherwise I cook myself some scrambled eggs."

"Then I want you to be here for Christmas so I can show you what it's really like! You'll come too, won't you, Hildy?"

"Well, I don't know . . ."

"Turkey, dressing"—Merry eyed Jack—"and at least four kinds of pie. I'll bake some and so will Hildy. Right?"

Jack smiled. The contrast from his normal demeanor was so pronounced that both women burst out laughing.

"We got him with the pies, Hildy," Merry joked, and the conversation turned to easy, idle chatter.

After Hildy left, Jack helped Merry carry dishes to the kitchen and load the dishwasher. Their shoulders brushed as he organized the plates and she placed the dirty glasses in the top basket. Merry was growing accustomed to this cozy domesticity.

Jack turned to leave and Merry asked, "What are you doing?"

"Me? I'm going to bed," Jack said, looking startled by the question.

"I'm not talking to you. I'm talking to my cat. Why is he following you?"

"Is there a rule against that?" Jack bent down and scratched the cat's head, producing a roaring purr from somewhere deep inside the feline.

"Nog never follows anyone around except me."

"You could have fooled me," Jack commented as he mounted another stair step with the cat on his heels. "I don't mind. He sleeps on my feet when he's in my room. And considering how cold it's been, it feels pretty good."

Merry's jaw dropped. "He sleeps with you?"

"I only let him in when he meows at my door. I didn't think you'd mind."

"No, I don't mind. It's just that . . ." Her voice trailed away. She did mind, actually. It wasn't that Jack was allowing the cat to sleep with him but that the cat even wanted to!

"Traitor," she muttered under her breath.

Chapter Eight

. . . .

"Uh-oh. Here comes trouble," Abby said as she looked out the window. There was a lull in the shopping frenzy, and both she and Merry were taking a breather.

Before Merry could ask more, the door to the shop slammed open and the baubles on the trees trembled from the impact. Regina Olsdorf roared in like a storm system and planted herself in front of Merry's till. Her face was dangerously red, and Merry wondered about the state of the woman's blood pressure.

Regina usually had her nose out of joint when she was distressed or offended, which was frequently. She was typically in a snit about one thing or another. Regina was a trying woman but also a good customer, one Merry didn't want to offend.

"Hi. Can I help you?" Merry sounded cheery even though the Olsdorf woman could put her teeth on edge. It took a lot to unhinge Merry's cheerfulness, but Regina managed it with ease.

"I certainly hope so. You're the closest to him." Regina's chin quivered indignantly, as if she could barely hold back her irritation.

"Him?"

"That man who's been staying here, of course." Regina could barely disguise her distaste at the mention of Jack's existence.

"Mr. Frost? What about him?"

"Is it true that he plans to take away people's homes and farmland?" Regina's face colored unattractively, in splotches. "That's despicable!"

Alarm bells went off in Merry's head. She fixed a blank expression on her features. "Take them away? I'm sure he wouldn't take anything that wasn't already his."

Regina eyed Merry suspiciously.

Abby hurried over with a cup of tea. "I've forgotten, Mrs. Olsdorf, do you take cream or sugar?"

"Sugar, dear." Regina beamed down upon Abby from her nearly six-foot height. Then she returned her gaze to Merry, the fire back in her eyes.

"He's snooping around at the courthouse in Blue Earth," Regina informed her, "and people don't like it. They're on fire!"

"Oh?" Merry kept her voice level. She was sure that Regina had talked to everyone she could get her hands on and fanned the flame.

"The people at the courthouse say he's very quiet, not friendly at all. I can't get anything out of the receptionist at his lawyer's office, but I know something is going on. Penny at the bank told me . . ."

"Regina, Penny likes to talk. Sometimes she speaks before she has her facts straight. I'm sure when the time is right you will hear about anything that affects you."

None of this likely pertained to Regina. She was simply making it her business, as she did most everything in Frost. Maybe she'd meet her match in Jack Frost, who seemed very capable of keeping private things private.

After a few more probing questions, which had disappointing results, Regina stuffed a handful of free peppermints into her purse and, without a good-bye, sailed out of the shop.

"That was interesting," Abby commented.

"I'm glad there were no other customers in here." Merry sank down on the stool behind the counter. "No one needs to hear speculation about my B-and-B guest."

"What *do* you think he's up to?"

"Who says he's up to something? He's inherited some land from his family. The *Frost* family. Seems to me he has a right to what's his."

"I don't know, Merry. I've heard some grumbling too. I hope there's no trouble."

Merry chewed worriedly on her lower lip. The residents of Frost might be up in arms if Jack's suspicions about his great-grandfather's property were true.

* * * * *

The store was so busy that Merry didn't even see Kipley Carson enter. Nor did she notice that he was carrying a single red rose.

"Kip!" She jumped when he put his hand on her shoulder and thrust the flower beneath her nose.

"Busy day?"

"Crazy." Merry pushed away an errant curl and smiled at him. "You, obviously, are not busy enough or you wouldn't be hanging around here. Is something wrong with the telephone company's business?" She gestured to the tools hanging on his belt.

"Who cares about business when I'm in Frost and I know you're in the store?" Kip's green eyes sparkled, and he ran his fingers through his rusty red hair.

"You're adorable, as usual, but you'll have to leave. I'm too busy to chat now. Can't you see?"

"You're in luck. I have work to do right here in town, and when I'm done I'll come back." He surprised her by kissing her on the forehead before handing her the rose. "See you soon."

As soon as the door shut behind him, the woman waiting at the counter said, "He's darling. Your boyfriend?"

"Kipley? No. We're just friends."

"Yeah. Right," Abby rejoined. "He's crazy in love with her and she can't see it."

"He is not," Merry said. "He's a friend."

"Every single man in a thirty-mile radius would like to be Merry's *friend*," Abby said in an aside to the woman.

"I heard that!" Merry shooed Abby toward some new customers who'd entered.

"Never mind her," she advised her customer.

"I saw the look that fellow gave you. He's infatuated with you."

Merry didn't have to respond to the comment because another group of shoppers came to the door, creating a commotion. She was thoughtful as she rang up gifts and decorations. Wearied from both thinking and working, when there was a lull in the store, she went to the kitchen and made herself a cup of tea.

Was she really so naïve that she didn't notice Kip's feelings? No, that wasn't it. She simply didn't want that complication in her life. She took the scripture very seriously that advised Christians not to be unequally yoked. She didn't date men who didn't have faith. What was the point? The relationship would go nowhere anyway.

Once, in college, she'd allowed that to happen and had fallen in love with an unbeliever. She'd regretted the pain it had caused ever since. Kip was fun and funny, but he wasn't the church-going type. Therefore, he wasn't her type either.

As if thinking about him could make him materialize, Kip appeared in the doorway, grinning.

"I'm done with work. What do you have to eat, Merry? Something good?" He sauntered in and settled himself at the table across from her. "You did invite me in, didn't you?"

"I must have." Merry smiled at him and reached for a container of cookies. "Here, help yourself."

"Want to go to a movie later?" he asked after four sugar cookies and a glass of milk. "You pick it. I'll even go to one of those stupid girlfriend movies if you want."

"Such sacrifice!" She poked his arm. "You know I can't. I don't take time off during December. There's too much going on here."

"All work and no play makes Merry a dull girl," he retorted with his most engaging smile. He put his hand over hers as it lay on the table. "Come on, Merry. For me?"

Jack chose that awkward moment to walk into the kitchen and see the couple holding hands. Merry withdrew hers, but it was too late. There was a guarded expression in Jack's eyes, one she hadn't seen before. He almost looked . . . angry.

She felt Kip stiffen at the sight of Jack, obviously not approving of a strange man walking into her kitchen.

"Kip, this is Jack," she said quickly. "He's my B-and-B guest."

"And who is Kip?" Jack inquired a little testily.

"He works for the telephone company."

"Very personal service, I see." Jack's voice was cool, insinuating, and Kip apparently didn't like it very much.

Kip half rose from his chair. He liked nothing better than a fight, and she could tell he didn't like Jack's tone. Merry jumped to her feet and dragged Kip with her.

"He was just going, weren't you, Kip?" She held onto his arm as she walked him to the door.

"I could clean his clock for you," Kip whispered. "I don't like this guy."

"You don't even know him," she hissed. "Now go home. And thanks for the rose."

"Just saying. Call me if he needs an attitude adjustment. I'd be happy to help."

She practically pushed Kip into the snow and slammed the door behind him. "Don't mind him. He's . . ." Merry stopped talking. Jack held the rose in his hand. He was studying the velvety petals ready to unfold.

"I didn't realize you had a boyfriend, Merry. I'm sorry I walked in like that." He seemed annoyed.

"He's not my boyfriend. Whatever Kip thinks or says,

he's got it wrong."

"You should give the guy a break, Merry. It would be a privilege to date a woman like you."

He left her standing there, gaping after him.

Chapter Nine

Jack paced back and forth across the floor of his room asking himself why he said what he did.

Because she had gotten under his skin, that's why. She was smart, happy, content. She wasn't needy or dependent but completely self-sufficient. And she was one of the loveliest women he'd ever met. With that blonde hair and those wide green eyes she was . . . angelic.

But where was she when he'd really needed an angel? Jack wondered. All those years of guilt and regret . . . and now she appears?

Nothing had made sense to him since he was twelve years old. *Why start now?* he thought bitterly.

Restless and not knowing what to do with himself, he flopped onto the bed and stared at the ornate ceiling fan light. For a man who'd cultivated a dispassionate, wary, guarded life, he was certainly letting his feelings run away with him. His long-gone relatives were driving him crazy. In fact, all of Frost was driving him insane. Frost and the woman downstairs . . .

When he'd seen her sitting at the table holding hands with that Kip fellow, he'd felt a surge of possessiveness he'd never before experienced. He was actually jealous! That was an emotion he'd left behind years ago—hadn't he?

Hours later, he awoke from a dream sweating. He sat straight up in bed, blinking back the saltiness that had slid into his eyes. He swung his legs over the bed, went to the bathroom sink, and threw cold water on his face until he was fully awake and the nightmare slithered back into his subconscious. It would raise its ugly head again later, no doubt, but not tonight.

It took him a long time to get back to sleep. It was the first time since he'd been in Frost that he'd had the recurrent dream that haunted him.

At 6:00 AM he could stay in bed no longer, even on a Sunday morning. Between his reaction to Merry and to the dream, he needed to move around, to erase thought and turn it into action.

Merry was at the kitchen table when he entered. Jack could tell she'd been crying. She rubbed at her eyes and gave him a watery smile.

"Coffee's ready," she volunteered.

He poured his own and sat down. "What's wrong?" He was surprised at how it hurt to see her this way.

"Don't mind me. I just get . . . sad . . . sometimes."

"Sad at Christmas? I thought it was your favorite time of year."

"It is now, but it wasn't always so. Some of my loneliest times were the holidays. I can't get Greta out of my mind. Poor little kid. Homeless at Christmas? How sad!"

"Then why don't you invite her family to spend Christmas here? I thought that's what you liked to do." He reached for a scone and began to munch on it. He was startled when Merry bolted out of her chair and flung her arms around his neck. She smelled of peppermint and sugar cookies.

"Of course! It certainly has to be better than a shelter." A frown creased her features. "You wouldn't mind, would you? I do have more than one room I use for the B-and-B. I doubt they'd bother you."

"I hope I'll be out of here by then."

"You *have* to stay through Christmas!" she insisted, her eyes bright with anticipation, tears gone. "You don't have other plans. What's a day or two more this time of year? Besides, it will be fun."

Then, as Merry was sometimes given to do, she changed subjects midstream.

"Do you want to go to church with me? It starts at nine."

"I don't usually go to church during December," he admitted. "Too much . . ."

". . . Christmas?"

"Sounds bad, doesn't it?"

"You must have your reasons." She eyed him steadily. "But I'd like company this morning. Will you break your rule just this once?"

Saying no to Merry was almost impossible, he'd learned. He didn't know how she managed it and hadn't seen it coming, but he heard himself say, "Just this once."

It was worth it to sit through Christmas carols just to see her face light up.

The church was a short walk from Merry's house. As they entered, it seemed that everyone there knew her. They probably did, Jack thought. There were less than two hundred people in this town—he'd read it on the sign when he'd driven in.

She greeted or hugged every person she met, and people seemed to gravitate to her like the sun. Merry was a people magnet, Jack decided. That was the last thing he'd ever wanted to be.

It felt like old times sitting in the pew, listening to Pastor Ed speak. The music from the organ, the old songs, the wavering voices of the elderly women in the congregation, the smell of coffee brewing in the basement—it all brought Jack back to his childhood.

He and Jamie had never been very well behaved in church, much to their parents' chagrin. Fortunately it seemed to amuse those sitting around them, which only encouraged their misbehaving. More than once, one of them was forced to sit in the back pew by himself. Both couldn't be sent back there. They'd have far too much fun. In spite of himself, Jack smiled.

* * * * *

"Let's think of something entertaining," Merry suggested when they returned from church. "Since neither of us works on Sundays, we might as well do something interesting."

Jack helped her out of her coat and hung it in the closet. "What did you have in mind?"

Things were getting rather chummy, Merry thought. They were acting like old marrieds this morning. She wasn't unhappy with the thought.

"We can go through the attic. I opened the heat registers so it will be warm up there. What's better on a snowy afternoon than going through old trunks and attic treasures? Today we're eating leftovers, so I don't even have to cook." She glanced at him. "If you don't mind, that is."

"Leftovers here are a gourmet dinner elsewhere," Jack said graciously. "But the attic is yours, you don't have to share it with me."

"It's your family's history. I'm sure there are things you'll want once you see them. Besides, I'll need you to interpret for me. Perhaps we'll find photographs of your ancestors. Come on, it will be fun!"

That's how they found themselves a half hour later, in jeans, bending low over a large antique steamer trunk in a warm, dusty attic, intent on breaking their way into the first of many chests and crates the room had to offer.

"Are you sure you want to break the lock? Maybe there's a key around here somewhere. I could look for it," Merry offered.

"That might take all day. Besides, I think I can do it without damaging the lock." Jack leaned his ear close to the padlock and began to move the dial to the right and then the left. In a matter of moments, the lock fell open in his hands.

"How did you do that?" Merry gasped.

"I learned it in my former life as a cat burglar."

She punched his arm and registered the strong, bunched muscles beneath his shirt.

"Actually, it was a skill Jamie and I perfected so that we'd have the run of the entire house—ours and everyone else's, for that matter."

"Naughty boy."

His smile was sad, as if there were no humor behind his thoughts. "I suppose you could say that."

She didn't pursue it because she didn't want to sound critical. They were comfortable with each other right now, and that had been something of a rarity during his stay.

She wanted to discover who this Jamie was but liked this easy companionship they shared for the moment, so she decided against it.

Jack lifted the trunk's lid to reveal a wealth of newspaper-wrapped items within. He picked one up, unwrapped it, and held up a fragile blue-and-white teacup. The dark blue color seemed to bleed through the porcelain to reveal itself on both sides of the plate.

"My mother had flow blue china too. She inherited it from her grandmother." Merry took the cup from Jack's hands to examine it.

Uninterested in dishes, he turned to another chest, one that opened easily. "What's this?" He withdrew a small body, the eyes of which were staring directly at him.

"She's beautiful!" Merry tenderly took the doll and, with a motion born of instinct, cradled it in her arms.

"There have to be a dozen dolls in here." Jack withdrew a marionette with tangled strings. "These must have belonged to my great-aunt. She didn't have any children to pass them down to."

"How sad," Merry murmured. "These dolls would make some little girl very happy."

The next words out of Jack's mouth shocked her. "Why don't you give them to Greta for Christmas?"

Tears welled in her eyes at the tender thought. "That's a beautiful suggestion, but I couldn't. Maybe someday you'll have little girls of your own. They are the ones who should have them."

Jack looked as if he'd never entertained such an idea. "Me? I . . . Then just pick one out for her if that worries you. She needs something nice."

For the first time since they'd met, Merry was absolutely sure that beneath that icy exterior beat a heart of gold.

"Pay dirt!" Merry crowed when Jack opened the third trunk. She lifted an old photo album out of the depths and laid it on the floor between them. Carefully she opened the cover.

The photos inside had been pasted onto the pages with paper corners, the glue on which had disintegrated long ago.

"Well, what do you know?" Jack picked up a photo of a somber-faced gentleman grimly staring at the camera. The Minneapolis Great Northern Depot loomed behind him. There was another of him at Navy Pier. "This is the man for whom Frost was named, and that's some of his work."

"He designed some very important buildings," Merry said, impressed. "Frost should be proud."

The next album she took from the trunk was considerably newer. She opened it and a familiar face stared back at her. "Jack, is this you?"

He leaned close, and his shoulder brushed hers. She was acutely aware of him. A pleasant little shiver flickered through Merry. Jack, however, seemed not to notice.

He studied the photo briefly. "That's my father. He's standing next to his aunt who owned this house."

"You look just like him. What a gorgeous man he is!" Merry realized what she'd said only after it was too late to stop herself.

Jack looked amused. "So are you saying that *I'm* gorgeous too?"

Merry's mouth worked but nothing came out. "I wasn't . . . I didn't . . . Well, yes, I guess I did. Please don't take offense!"

"Offense? Hardly. I should kiss you for a compliment like that . . ." Now it was Jack's voice that faded as they stared at each other.

He cleared his throat. "Now it's your turn to be offended. I didn't mean . . ."

Merry laughed. "Touché, now we're even."

"Awkward begets awkward, I guess." His smile was genuine.

She returned to the album and flipped the page. There were more photos of Jack's father and his aunt, then some with a slender, beautiful woman in a white dress. Her dark hair curled around her face, and she was laughing. Merry held out the album to Jack.

"My mother." He said nothing more.

"She's stunning. Was she a model or an actress?"

"No. Just a mother."

It was odd, the way he said it. He obviously didn't want to discuss her further.

The next page held a family photo. She immediately recognized Jack's parents. With them were two young boys dressed in matching shorts and shirts. Their knees were scuffed but every hair on their heads was plastered into place. One grinned widely while the other looked somberly into the camera.

Merry handed the photo to Jack. "Is this your family?"

He stiffened at the sight of it. His features grew ashen, and his jaw set in a hard line. "Yes." Jack laid the album aside.

"What darling boys. Are you a twin?"

"No." He hesitated before adding, "Yes. Just not anymore."

Merry's heart twisted in her chest. "Oh, I'm sorry. He passed away?"

"Yes." His voice was toneless.

"Can you tell me about it?" As usual, Merry went where lesser angels dared to tread. "I know how it is to lose someone . . . my parents . . ."

He stared straight ahead, his face expressionless. "I prefer not to talk about it."

Her face crumpled, and tears sprang to her eyes. "I'm so sorry. I shouldn't have pried. I have such a big mouth. . . ."

He put his hand on hers to stop her. "It's not your fault. You didn't know."

"That doesn't matter. I suppose it was because we were sitting here in the attic, chatting like friends. I just . . ."

Jack put his hands on her shoulders and turned her so she faced him. "Forget it, okay? It's nearly five. How about taking a break and going out for dinner? Your choice of restaurants, my treat."

"Really?" She brightened. "That would be wonderful."

"Consider it done."

"Give me ten minutes to replace my makeup." Merry jumped to her feet and wiped away a tear that had coursed down one cheek. Someday she'd learn to keep her mouth shut, but obviously it wasn't today.

* * * * *

The restaurant in Mankato was nearly full when they arrived, and they were escorted to a horseshoe-shaped back booth. The waitress put the menus side by side in the center of the U-shaped banquette. Merry scooted into the seat from one side and Jack the other. That left them side by side, shoulders touching, staring out into the main dining room.

"Want to see something cool?" The waitress pulled the decorative green velvet curtain that lined the back of the booth so that it partially encircled the table. "That's for privacy. The owner's wife comes for dinner and they always sit here to get a little privacy. Sometimes she does bookwork here as well. I suppose they have to grab time together when they can. The restaurant business is pretty demanding. The small redhead grinned. "The two of you look like you need some nice personal time. I'll be back shortly to take your orders." She pulled the curtain closed a little more before she left them.

"The things you learn!" Merry commented. "I don't know if we should be embarrassed or flattered that she thought we were . . . you know."

"A couple?" There was amusement on Jack's features. "Maybe we should be flattered."

Merry hid her reddening face in the oversized menu and pretended to read. She was grateful that things went smoothly from the salad through the entrée.

Only when the dishes had been whisked away and replaced by dessert menus did an awkward silence develop.

"What's your favorite?" Jack asked, indicating the list of sweets.

"All of them, of course, but I especially love their bread pudding and apple tarts."

Jack ordered one of each and a pot of coffee. After the dessert, he leaned back on the bench and took a deep breath.

"Merry, I've been thinking. You deserve an explanation about my response to that photo earlier. I didn't intend to be rude. Frankly, I rarely talk about my brother, Jamie."

"You don't have to now, either. It was terribly hard to discuss my parents' deaths for a long time. It was a terrible shock to me. Please don't . . ."

He put his hand on hers. "Let me tell you. You should know."

He ran a finger along the inside of his collar as if it were suddenly too tight. "Jamie was my younger brother by ten minutes," he said softly. "He was nearly a pound lighter than me, so I got the moniker of big brother even though only minutes separated us in age." His eyes focused on a spot somewhere back in time.

"Were you close?"

"We finished each other's sentences, had the same ideas at the same time, and could practically read each other's minds. My father told me it was eerie sometimes, how much we were alike. Jamie caught up to me in size quickly, and very few people were able to tell us apart."

"Even your parents?"

"They had their ways. I don't remember how old I was when I realized that the barber always cut our hair slightly differently. If you look at that photo again, my hair is cut shorter around the ears. It's nothing the general populace would notice, but it kept Mom and Dad from mixing us up."

"Very clever." Merry smiled widely. "If I ever have identical twins I'll have to remember that."

"Also remember that when they're old enough to take themselves to the barber, they can have their hair cut any way they want."

"You didn't!"

"We did. The barbershop was only a couple blocks from our house, so we started walking there together when we were quite small. My parents never considered that we might fool the barber as well. Jamie and I switched haircuts back and forth until no one but Jamie and I knew who we were."

"Did they suspect?" Merry covered her mouth with her hand, trying not to laugh, imagining the confusion and chaos the two boys created.

"They suspected we were up to something but weren't sure what it was. They figured it out when we were twelve. Jamie and I thought it was a shame. We'd hoped to continue our charade into high school so we could mess with the teachers." He smiled faintly. "I think the term they used for us was 'incorrigible.'"

"What about girls?"

"We were too young for girls back then, but we had that planned too. We would each date the same girl, and if one of us liked her we could claim her. We weren't very sophisticated at that age, so we didn't even consider what the poor girls might think."

"Did you do it?" Merry inquired, thinking how she'd feel if one of the boys she'd dated turned out to be someone else entirely.

"No. We never did." He looked at Merry intently. "Jamie died before then. I killed him."

Chapter Ten

Merry grew very still. All the air seemed to have been sucked out of the curtained cocoon in which they sat. She wound her fingers together in her lap, helpless to do anything else with them. She wanted to reach out, to tell him he was surely mistaken, that his imagination had run away with him, but she didn't. The ring of surety and truth in his voice had been too convincing.

Jack didn't relieve the tension by speaking. He was lost in his emotions. Sadness, regret, guilt, and blame, by turn, skimmed across his features. There was no jest in his words. Finally he looked at her. His eyes appraised her, as if he were measuring how she was taking the information.

If he'd planned to find any judgment or censure there, he was disappointed.

Merry felt compassion flood through her. If Jamie had died when he was twelve, then Jack was also twelve. Whatever blame he'd taken upon himself, Jack couldn't have caused his brother's death. But to carry that belief, that burden, for more than twenty years? That was a second tragedy—two lives affected, not just one.

"You aren't going to say anything?" Jack sounded surprised, as if not everyone had taken the news with such composure.

"I'm so sorry about your brother's death, Jack. But I don't believe . . ."

"Believe it. I killed my brother." His voice was flat, as if he'd practiced saying the words until he could utter them without sentiment.

She couldn't speak. Merry simply stared at him and prayed for help from above.

"So now you know."

"I know nothing, Jack, except that your brother must have died a tragic death that you, at twelve, blamed yourself for."

"I don't just blame myself. I did it. I pushed my own brother to his death."

The waitress arrived with their desserts at that inopportune time.

Jack looked up and said calmly, "If you don't mind, Merry, can we take these to go? I don't feel much like eating right now."

The waitress disappeared with the dishes and quickly returned with take-out containers. Jack threw money on the table, far more than the bill would amount to, and stood.

Merry collected the white Styrofoam boxes, and they moved quickly to the front of the restaurant and out the door.

Jack turned the key in the ignition, backed the car from its parking space, and swung it around. He sped out of town. The only sound that could be heard was that of bits of gravel spraying the underside of the vehicle.

She watched his stoic profile in the glow of the dashboard and ached inside.

When he finally began to speak, he seemed to be recounting the events for himself more than for her, digging at the wound.

"Jamie and I were always looking for adventure," he said softly. "We had no fear—and no common sense, either. We'd spent our young lives looking for the next thrill—tubing on the river, stuffing frogs in girls' lockers, skipping school to go to the arcade, trying to do dangerous jumps at the local skating rink, skiing black diamonds when we had instructions from our parents to stay on the bunny hill."

Merry shivered at the very idea. How must it have been for the mother of these two wild, rambunctious children? Heart-stopping, no doubt.

"The only thing we'd never done a lot of was sledding. There's not much of that in California, at least not where we lived. But one Christmas holiday, my parents took us to the mountains. We had a great time, Jamie and I. By then, my parents had given up trying to tame us, and the entire staff at the resort knew our names. That's how we managed to check out a sled."

Something twisted in Merry's gut, and she realized this was a story that would end badly.

"We spent the morning sliding down the designated hills, but after a while that became boring. So, without permission, Jamie and I took our sleds to a steeper hill to give that a try." The light from the dash played on Jack's even features and revealed the effort it took to tell this story.

"Jamie always wanted to go first at anything we tried. Sometimes we fought about that, but not that day. It was Christmas Eve, and I suppose I thought I'd be generous to the little squirt this once.

"He was balanced at the top of the hill, the front of his sled already hanging over the edge, when our parents saw us. They were running toward us with one of the ski instructors and yelling at us to stop. Since that had never slowed us down before, and Jamie was afraid he wouldn't get to try this if we listened, he asked me to push him. Better to ask for forgiveness than permission was Jamie's philosophy. 'Hurry up, Jack! I'll never get to try this if I don't do it now,' Jamie said."

Jack paused and then said, "And I *pushed* him!"

His voice broke, and it was some time before he could speak again. "He just lay there at the bottom of the hill, like a broken toy. I don't know what happened. He must not have been strong enough to steer the sled away from that tree. I didn't think he was aimed in that direction or I never would have given the sled a push . . ."

"Oh, Jack," Merry said helplessly.

"When I finally looked back, someone had radioed for help. Dad was running toward an easier path down the hill, and my mother had sunk to her knees in the snow. It all happened so quickly, I couldn't take it in. Jamie had to be fooling around, I thought, pretending to be hurt in order to scare us all." Jack took a deep breath. "But he wasn't joking."

"Then what?" Merry whispered. She felt for that twelve-year old Jack, the confusion, the terror, and finally, the guilt.

"An ambulance came but they couldn't drive down the hill. Finally several men carried Jamie out on a stretcher. It probably took twenty minutes, but it seemed like twenty years. I kept waiting for Jamie to jump up, but he never did. And my mother just kept sobbing."

Jack's voice had grown low, and he was completely immersed in the memory.

"We went to the hospital but didn't get to see him for a long time. When we did, he was on life support. My parents wanted me to go back to the hotel and rest, but of course I couldn't. We stayed at the hospital that night. I never did sleep. I just kept willing Jamie to wake up. I also prayed that God would make this all go away, that He would take us back to the moment before I pushed that sled, but God did neither."

Merry closed her eyes, and tears leaked from beneath her lids and coursed down her cheeks.

"In the morning, three doctors came in and told my parents that Jamie had no brain activity and that they recommended taking him off life support. We said our goodbyes and then Jamie was gone."

"On Christmas Day?"

"Yes." He turned to her and the pain in his expression seemed as fresh as if the accident had just happened. "So now maybe you can understand why Christmas is not a time for celebration for me. And when I say I killed my brother, I really did."

"Jack, you were a child! It could just as well have been you on that sled. It was an accident!"

Merry was going to continue when she realized they were parked in her own driveway. Where had the time and the miles gone? "Come inside," she said gently. "No use sitting out here."

He followed her into the house, where they both shed their coats. Jack began to prowl about like a restless lion in too small a cage.

Merry let him pace until he finally settled in a large wing chair by the fireplace. Then she sat down across from him. "Tell me about your mother."

"Before or after my brother died?" Jack asked bleakly. "Both."

"She was very traditional, very proper, a lady. She was accustomed to having things her own way. That comes with having money, I guess. But she always said that her twins were the ones who taught her to loosen up, to relax. She couldn't have power over us like she controlled others, so she finally had to accept that we were a force to be reckoned with and enjoyed. She became a lot of fun after that. My father was the disciplinarian, and Mom sometimes even consorted with us in our tricks and mischief." He smiled faintly. "Those were good times."

"And after?"

"My mother just . . . disappeared. It was as if she faded before our eyes. No more laughter, no more smiles. It took everything in her just to keep herself together. She took medication until her eyes glazed over, saw therapists until their names all ran together, and spent the rest of the time locked in her room. She was kind to me but distant. After all, I'd killed her son."

"You were her son too! You didn't kill anyone."

Jack shifted in his chair, crossed one long leg over the other, and finally seemed to see her. "No? I guess no one else blamed me, but I blame myself. I should have known better. I should have stopped Jamie."

"You were *twelve*! Do you know any twelve-year-old boys with the common sense of an experienced adult? I don't think so!"

"Maybe not, but I grew up thinking I should have been the exception."

"You always talk about your mother in past tense," Merry observed. "Is she . . . ?"

"She died four years after Jamie. It was as if she just couldn't muster up the will to live once he was gone. Like I said, she faded away. She grew quieter and thinner. She slept less and paced the house at night. One day my father found her in bed—gone. Just like that she disappeared completely from my life, without a word, without a good-bye."

He skewered her with a look that held her rapt. "And that, Merry, is why I can't celebrate Christmas. It was the beginning of the end for my family. I know God is the one who carried me through those bad years or I probably wouldn't be here either, but that doesn't mean I like all the brouhaha and manic glee I see around Christmas. Quite frankly, I despise it."

Despise was a pretty heavy word to use for the things Merry loved about the holiday. It hurt her, but at least now she understood why he was so adamant about his feelings.

She tucked her feet beneath her on the couch and pulled an afghan over her lap. It felt cool in the house despite the fire. Or perhaps it was just the flame of excitement she felt about the holidays being extinguished.

"Thank you for telling me, Jack. I know it was difficult for you. At least now I understand why . . . you are the way you are." She pulled on a lock of golden hair that had strayed from behind her ear. "But even though your feelings are real and your story tragic, it doesn't mean you should keep other people from taking pleasure in the birth of the Savior. Granted, some go too far and forget the real meaning of Christmas, but it's also a wonderful time to spread the Good Word. Everyone identifies with the baby in the manger."

"I just can't help it, Merry. It's like a knife in my heart when I see elves and reindeer and hear silly songs about Rudolph or Frosty. Christmas is a matter of life or death for me on so many levels. It's the beginning of the end for my family and for Christ who also had to die."

"It's not my place to judge you, Jack. I respect your views. You earned them the hard way. You lost so much. You don't have to agree, but you do have to understand that there is more than one way to approach a subject."

He studied her somberly. "Agree to disagree, you mean?"

"Something like that."

"And quit trying to impose my views on Frost?"

"Please."

"I can't promise you that, Merry. I will say that whatever property doesn't belong to me can stay as it is. As for my land and property, I don't want it to be Santa's runway anymore, okay?"

She could agree to that. Thankfully her house wasn't under Jack's ownership. At least Merry's Christmas Boutique was safe.

Chapter Eleven

....

"Do you like horses?"

Jack looked up from his breakfast, startled. "I suppose so. I've done some riding but never had the time to keep it up. I had a friend who owned a ranch. We lost touch, and I didn't continue riding. That was a long time ago."

Merry sat down across from him. "I have a friend who has horses too. I've been thinking of organizing a sleigh ride. Are you interested?"

"Sounds a little too Christmassy for me. Thanks for asking though." He went back to his eggs.

"I'm asking for a reason. I've been trying to think of a way to do something nice for Greta and her family, something that involves others. I know sleigh rides border on having the Christmas spirit, but these people may not have a real Christmas so why not a memorable holiday event?"

She looked straight into his eyes. "Frankly, I need people who know the situation and will make them feel comfortable. Abby and her husband have agreed to come and so have my pastor and his wife. With Greta's family, me, and my friend Jeff, who owns the horses, that makes nine people. A full sleigh is ten. So if you'd agree, I wouldn't have to look for someone else to fill that last spot."

Jack squirmed a little so she hurried to add, "Besides, it will be fun. Jeff has beautiful horses, and he's got a wonderful voice. We can sing carols and—and—" She stammered to a stop, realizing what she'd just suggested. "Or not."

Much to her amazement, without any argument whatsoever, Jack said, "I'll do it. For that little girl. Not because it's Christmas."

"Deal." Merry extended a hand to shake.

When his fingers encased hers in a strong grip, she felt fragile and delicate. The handshake seemed as personal as an embrace. She pulled away and averted her eyes.

"Good. I'll count on you then. Tomorrow night after you come back from Blue Earth."

She quickly escaped the kitchen, but she felt Jack's gaze boring into her back.

* * * * *

Now why had he gone and done that? Jack gripped the steering wheel of his rental car as he drove toward Blue Earth. The road was icy, and the last thing he needed was to go into the ditch. Everything he was finding out at the courthouse was giving him fits, and he didn't need more trouble.

But he'd already generated more trouble. He'd agreed to go on a sleigh ride, of all things. Why had he . . . ?

It wasn't hard to figure out the answer. He'd said yes because he wanted to get a good look at Merry's friend Jeff.

She'd dropped Jeff's name enough times in casual conversation to make him curious. He felt oddly protective of her, this woman who wore her heart on her sleeve and would give everything she had if she thought someone needed it. She'd treated him far better than he'd deserved those first couple days he was in Frost. He appreciated that more than she could know.

It was really going to happen, this sleigh ride, Jack observed as he arrived at Merry's Christmas Boutique at six the next evening. There were two huge Percheron horses hooked to something that looked like a large open box on runners. It was filled with soft mounds of loose hay and piles of cozy blankets.

The regal-looking horses stood at least nineteen hands high and had to weigh a ton or more each. Their large, prominent eyes seemed to take in everything, and they stood surprisingly still considering the excitement around them.

Greta was particularly rambunctious, running alongside the horses from their noses to their tails and then back again. Her mother was trying to convince the little girl to stand still but to no avail. Abby and her husband, Charley, were chatting with Pastor Ed Nordstrom and his wife, Betty. Merry, dressed in a green down coat and red Santa's hat, carried thermoses and plastic containers full of food to the rig. She handed the parcels up to a ruggedly good-looking man with three days' worth of grizzled stubble, short and slightly tousled hair, and a wide white grin—especially when he smiled down at Merry. He wore jeans and a thick buffalo plaid jacket. On the wagon seat lay a fur hat—flaps and all—and a pair of thick gloves.

Nothing to criticize there, Jack realized. This guy was perfect for the role he was playing tonight. He was the rugged horseman, impervious to cold and snow and obviously smitten with Merry. She, however, seemed oblivious to Jeff's flirtatious smiles.

Jack was overdressed in his suit jacket and highly polished shoes. He waved at the group and ducked into the house to change clothes. The night was getting cold fast.

"Come meet Greta and her parents," Merry ordered when he returned. "You know Abby and Charley and remember Pastor Ed and Betty from church." She made introductions and pointed at Jeff, who was up on the seat. "These horses are Jeff's gorgeous girls. Aren't they something?" She pointed to the horses, which Jack noticed had large red bows fastened to the tops of their tails.

Merry counted off her list on her fingers. "Cocoa, graham crackers, marshmallows, and chocolate . . ."

"We're going to have s'mores?" Greta screeched with delight.

"And tuna sandwiches with chips to eat while we ride. Oh yes, and music." She produced an old battery-operated radio that looked as though it should have been put in the garbage twenty-five years earlier.

Jack tried to stay out of the way of the merrymakers— who were enjoying this adventure far more than he—by burrowing into a mound of hay inside the rim of bales Jeff had placed around the perimeter of the sleigh.

He might have succeeded in going unnoticed had not Greta chosen him to be her new best friend.

* * * * *

Greta had cornered Jack, Merry noticed. Good for her. Let him try to be the Grinch around such a child! Discreetly Merry edged her way closer to the pair so she could hear what Greta was saying.

The little girl shook him by the shoulder until he looked at her. Then, with eyes so round they looked like full moons, she asked, "Are you really Jack Frost? Miss Merry read a book about Jack Frost at school."

"She did, did she?" Jack shot Merry a questioning glance.

She was glad for the darkness, which hid the blush creeping up her neck and across her cheeks.

"He was friends with Frosty the Snowman and Rudolph the red-nosed reindeer." Greta leaned closer to Jack. "Do you really know Frosty?"

Merry stifled a giggle. Then an unpleasant thought struck her. She hoped Jack wouldn't disappoint Greta with his answer.

"Well, the thing is . . ." He cleared his throat as if stalling for time.

Merry stiffened.

"The thing is that I live in California, Greta, and it's very warm in California all year long. Frosty hates that kind of weather, so he's never in the state."

"Oh." Greta sounded disappointed, but she bounced back quickly. "How can you freeze things if you live in California?"

Jack cleared his throat. "Frosty doesn't like to fly on airplanes, but I do."

Greta's face cleared. "So if you want to, you can go to cold places!"

"I'm here right now, aren't I?"

The little girl clapped her hands. "And that's why we have icicles!"

Merry was delighted. Jack hadn't lied exactly, nor had he disappointed the child with his answer.

As Merry turned away, she saw Greta climbing onto Jack's lap. "Can you tell me about the North Pole? Just how big are the elves anyway?"

Merry turned her attention to Greta's mother and stepfather. The young couple sat close together, leaning on a bale and holding hands through bulky mittens. "How are you doing?"

"It's so good to get out and do something fun for a change." Stephanie turned to her husband, whom she'd introduced as Wayne. "Isn't it, honey?"

Wayne nodded somberly. "We've had a string of really bad luck lately. Neither of us have found jobs yet, and we couldn't pay the rent so we lost our place. We are so grateful to the shelter to let us stay there and keep Greta in school. Anyway, it's good to laugh again. Thanks for having us."

"Greta talks about you at school. I thought you two could use a break."

Stephanie and Wayne exchanged glances. "We're grateful for the help we've been given. I've been doing some job interviews," Wayne said. "I think I'll be able to find something in Blue Earth. Then we can look for housing."

"And I'll look for work," Stephanie added. "We have bills to pay, and Greta could certainly use some clothing that didn't come from secondhand stores and rummage sales."

"I wish you all the best," Merry said with all her heart.

Then Pastor Ed weighed in on the conversation. "I told them I thought the church could help them with groceries. And our janitor is complaining more and more about his knees and how he needs one replaced. I told Wayne that he should apply for the job to fill in while Melvin is recovering. Every little bit helps."

"How kind!" Stephanie's forehead creased. "But when we get on our feet, I want to give back any way I can."

"It's a deal," Pastor Ed said. "Thank you."

Stephanie favored him with a satisfied smile.

"Tell me more about yourselves," Pastor Ed encouraged.

"There's not much to tell," Stephanie said. "We've been married two years and, as you can tell, we haven't had an easy start. I was in a bad state when I met Wayne, but we've finally gotten past all that. When my first husband died . . . Losing him brought me to my knees. If it weren't for the fact I had to take care of Greta and that I met Wayne, I'm not sure what would have happened to me. I thank God that He found me and lifted me out of the morass my life had become, before I made it even worse. . . ." Stephanie grew silent and pensive.

Merry wished the woman would continue but sensed that Greta's mother had already said more than she'd meant to. Her heart ached for the young woman who'd already suffered so much. What else had Stephanie endured?

Jack, Stephanie, Hildy—they all had secrets they were reluctant to share.

Merry's attention drifted to the conversation Jack was having with Greta. She had to admit he was a great sport about Greta's fascination with him.

"He also likes to play tricks on people," Jack was saying, referring to his namesake, "like cold toes and fingers. Have you ever had those?"

"Oh yes." The child's eyes were big as the moon. "You did that?"

Merry smiled to herself and cuddled deep beneath her blanket.

The crunch of the snow under the runners of the sleigh, the jingle of bells, and the soft sounds of the horses lulled them all into a tranquil silence.

About thirty minutes into the ride, Merry struggled to her feet and moved toward Jeff on the driver's seat.

"How's it going?"

"Good." He looked down at her with a smile. "Do you want to hike up here with me?"

Merry didn't see Jack staring at her in the darkness or the expression of displeasure on his features as she scrambled onto the seat beside Jeff.

"That's more like it," he said, pleasure in his voice. "You know I always like it best when you're by my side."

"Sweet talk won't get you anywhere with me," Merry informed him cheerily as she grabbed a blanket and put it over her knees.

"Tell me about it." Jeff's voice was warm, throaty, and intimate, as if they were alone in the world. "What *will* get to you, Merry? I've tried everything I know."

"Be my friend."

"I am your friend."

"Good!" she said delightedly. "Because, if you are my friend, you won't pursue this conversation any longer. Right?"

Jeff groaned but then leaned over and kissed Merry's cheek. "Okay, keep playing hard to get. I'm a patient man."

They rode in silence until she abruptly lifted her hands to the sky. "Look at all the stars! How amazing it is! It's like the Bible says, 'He also made the stars. God set them in the vault of the sky to give light on the earth to govern the day and the night, and to separate light from darkness. And God saw that it was good.' Neat, huh?"

Jeff was too busy to answer. He directed the horses to stop, jumped down, held out his hands to Merry, lifted her off the seat, and planted her on the snowy ground.

The others stood up, curious, and looked around.

Jeff quickly lit the campfire he'd apparently built earlier and began helping the others to the ground.

There were split logs in a circle around the fire, a stash of sticks peeled and pointed on one end for marshmallows, and a red-and-white cooler on the ground.

Greta ran around the log circle squealing with delight. "A bonfire! A bonfire!"

She came up to Merry. "I've heard of a bonfire, Miss Merry, and I saw a picture, but I never thought I'd get to see a real one!"

"Sometimes the simple things are the best." Merry started at the sound of Jack's voice in her ear.

"Yes. Greta reminds me of that all the time. I'll never take a bonfire for granted again." Merry smiled up into his eyes and noticed the tender expression on his face. Feeling a little off center at his look, she added, "You can be the first to help Greta roast a marshmallow. She adores you, you know."

"*Adore* is a pretty strong word, but I will agree she *likes* me." He chuckled as if recognizing the irony in his next statement. "Of course, who wouldn't? I'm a winter celebrity around here." Then he reached for one of the sticks and took a marshmallow out of the bag Jeff was passing around.

While he and Greta roasted marshmallows, Merry stood back, evaluating her feelings.

She liked Jeff. She really did. But she was also cautious because she knew herself too well. What she loved was the idea of family, kids, relatives, relationships. If she were honest, she loved that idea more than any of the men she had dated. She couldn't rush into marriage just for the family unit it would bring.

The man she married had to be the most important thing. Until she could trust herself to discern that she was in love for love's sake and nothing else, would she settle down? Jeff's family was big, rowdy, and fun. But was that enough reason to marry Jeff? Hardly. Only time would help her sort out her feelings for him or for any of the men who currently pursued her.

It was all too complicated. *She* was all too complicated. Until someone came along and was willing to sort this out with her, she would remain single.

Then she realized that several people were yelling just outside the ring of light thrown by the fire. She hurried over to find Greta and Jack making huge wet snow angels, their arms and legs spreading and closing gracefully, creating the look of bodies with full skirts and wings on the pristine palette of snow.

Merry wondered if that counted as a miracle, Jack playing in the snow with the child. He'd as much as said he didn't even *like* fun. Yet here he was, having plenty.

"Miss Merry, come and make a snow angel!" Greta called.

Impulsively, Merry dropped to the ground beside Greta and began to move her arms and legs in graceful arcs. Their laughter capped the festive mood.

Greta and Jack rolled a snowman while Merry set out the food, and after they'd eaten, Jeff brought out his guitar and they began to sing Christmas carols. Pastor Ed's low, rumbly voice led them. Stephanie had a sweet, clear soprano, and the others followed along.

Jack didn't even issue a complaint.

He was a different man tonight, Merry observed. For once he'd let down his guard and allowed himself to actually enjoy the music. He was even smiling, which warmed her heart. No one should spend his or her life in such emotional pain. If only there were some way she could help . . .

The ride home was quiet, each pondering the evening, deep in their own thoughts. Greta immediately fell asleep on her mother's lap. Merry found herself beside Jack. She was enormously gratified by the way things had turned out and grateful to Jack that he'd made the evening so much fun for Greta. He wasn't such a bad guy, just a little skittish about the holidays. Not that she could blame him. She had her own childhood issues about the season—and she hadn't lost a twin brother.

Her guests dispersed immediately upon returning to the boutique.

"All that fresh air wore us out," Pastor Ed announced as his wife yawned. "We'll all sleep well tonight."

Even Jeff was tired and eager to get his team home, so he departed with the rest of them. That left Jack and Merry on the top step waving good-bye to the group.

"Thanks for bullying me into going, Merry. It was more fun than I expected," Jack said.

"You're welcome. Greta is crazy about you."

"Sweet little girl. Nice parents. Too bad they've had so much trouble." He studied her face in the moonlight. "And it was very thoughtful of you to plan an outing with them in mind. You're very considerate, Merry." He wore just a hint of a smile. "I like that in a woman."

And he disappeared into the house, leaving Merry on the step staring after him in stunned surprise.

Chapter Twelve

It was ten o'clock and Jack hadn't come down for breakfast. Merry was glad she'd decided on French toast this morning. Anything else would have been burned to a crisp by now. She put the orange juice back into the refrigerator, wiped the already clean countertops, and put a jug of apple cider and spices on to heat for the afternoon customers. Still no Jack.

Maybe he hadn't planned to go to Blue Earth today and just forgot to tell her.

But Jack never forgot anything. His mind was like the proverbial steel trap. It was also part of his problem. He still remembered every detail of his brother's death, unable to erase it from his mind. The story was fresh every day for Jack, and he'd been living with that all his life.

At eleven, Merry decided to take matters into her own hands. Surely the man wouldn't sleep for more than twelve hours . . . would he?

She straightened out her Christmas moose sweater and brushed the front of her green corduroys, pushed her pale hair behind her ears, and pulled back her shoulders. Mind made up, she headed for the second floor bedroom where Jack slept.

She raised her hand to knock on his door, but before she could, she heard a rough, grating cough inside the room. Merry tested the doorknob. Unlocked. "Jack?" she ventured. Another cough. She pushed the door ajar.

"It's Merry. Can I bring your breakfast up to you? It will be noon soon, and I imagine you want to get to Blue Earth."

Jack mumbled something that sounded like "water."

"Excuse me, but I didn't quite get what you said. Did you want water? I can bring up some cold bottles if . . ." She pushed open the door and came to a complete stop.

Jack was still in bed. Every blanket, throw, and coverlet in the room was piled on top of him, the fireplace was roaring, and when she checked the thermostat, it was set on eighty-five degrees.

Always so put together and unruffled, this was a new Jack. His hair was sleep tousled, his face flushed, and his forehead beaded with sweat.

Her substantial nurturing instincts coming to the fore, Merry crossed the room and put her hand on his forehead. He was burning up. And despite the stiflingly hot room and heaps of covers, he was also shivering uncontrollably.

When she touched his cheek, he opened his eyes. "Sick," he muttered, stating what was already supremely obvious to Merry.

She hurried into the bathroom and began to run cold water in the sink. When she'd soaked a washcloth in the icy water, rung it out, and picked up a container of bottled water, she returned to Jack's bedside. She laid the cold rag on his forehead and he winced slightly, as if the cold pained him. Then she opened the water bottle and, with her hand supporting his shoulders, made him drink.

She felt like she'd touched a hot fireplace poker as she withdrew her arm. He must have a temperature of at least 104.

"I'm going to call my doctor," she announced in the direction of the bed.

"I just need some sleep."

"If your temperature gets any higher, you're going to need the fire department. In fact, that might be a good idea. I'm going to call the ambulance."

"No!"

"Then I'll take you to the clinic." She said it firmly, not believing for a minute that the man could even stand up.

There was nothing but a groan from the bed.

Merry marched down the stairs and called the clinic.

"Sounds like he needs to be seen," the nurse informed Merry. "If he can't get here on his own, you'll have to call the ambulance. Do you have a thermometer?"

"Somewhere. I can dig it out."

"Take his temperature and call me back."

"Okay," Merry said hesitantly. The woman might as well have said to wake a grizzly bear from hibernation and stick a thermometer in its mouth.

It took her several minutes to unearth the thermometer. When she returned to Jack's room, she was surprised to see him sitting on the bed. He'd dressed in jeans and a sweatshirt but his feet were bare. He was sweating profusely, as if the labor of getting dressed had taken every ounce of his strength.

And it probably had, Merry thought. Jack looked, as her mother used to say, "like death warmed over."

"What's this? You're up."

"I'm not going anywhere in an ambulance." His voice was low and throaty, and it sounded as if it hurt him to talk.

"Then you'll let me take you to the doctor?"

"I told you, I just need more sleep."

She brandished the thermometer in his face. "We'll do this. If your temp is under 102 degrees, you can stay here. If it's more, we go to the doctor. Now open up."

* * * * *

"Your thermometer has to be wrong," Jack muttered as they drove toward Blue Earth. He was perspiring again but still shivering. She'd warmed up the car, given him three blankets to put over his legs, and insisted on his bundling up like a child going outside to build a snowman.

Thankfully the exertion of getting dressed and into the car had worn him out, and he fell asleep almost immediately. She knew he would have complained for eleven and a half miles if he were awake. She glanced over at him and smiled. In repose, he looked younger, and she could imagine the little boy that he'd been. Without the tension of responsibilities showing on his features, he was incredibly handsome, so unlike the legend of Jack Frost, the imaginary sprite that had managed to haunt him his entire life.

His lips were parted, his features flushed, and his long dark eyelashes fanned out from his closed eyes. Merry's heart jolted unexpectedly at the affection she felt for him. To her dismay, she realized she also felt a less welcome emotion—attraction.

That would have to stop. He was a transient guest in her home and a potential source of pain and trouble for a number of people she counted as friends. There could be nothing serious between them. They were on opposite sides of the fence over what should happen to Frost . . . and Christmas.

They needed a wheelchair to get him into the clinic because Jack's knees kept buckling when he walked, and he was immediately put in an examination room.

"Stay with him till the doctor comes in, okay?" the

middle-aged nurse with a compassionate smile said. "I don't want him passing out and hurting himself."

"I don't need a babysitter," Jack muttered, but he also didn't tell Merry to leave the room.

When the doctor arrived, Merry stood up to leave. She felt Jack's hand on her arm. "Stay."

She dropped back into her chair, surprised by his request.

Dr. Henderson was a brisk, efficient, and dedicated physician. It didn't take him long to make his assessment of Jack. "We'll do x-rays, but my guess is he has double pneumonia and a nasty virus going on. In fact, we can do the x-rays in the hospital once we admit him. I'll put him on some . . ." Henderson began doctor-speak about medications and their dosages.

"No hospital," Jack croaked.

"You could also have strep throat," the doctor said as if he hadn't even heard Jack. "Your throat is raw. We'll run a test for that as well. I'll send the nurse in to help you get admitted."

"No . . ." Jack protested, but the doctor was already gone.

"It's okay," Merry assured him. "You'll get better more quickly with IVs and good care. It's much better than lying around my house until you have no choice but to call for help."

"You'll be late for work," he said, surprising her.

"Thank you for thinking of me, but I called Abby. She's taking care of things at the store. And there's no school today. That's why Greta got to stay up so late last night. Oh dear. Do you think making snow angels with Greta had anything to do with it? It had to be chilly on the ground."

The nurse entered with several papers and directions to hospital admissions, and there was no more conversation.

Later, Merry re-read the same *Arthritis Today* magazine for the third time as she sat in the hospital family room. She wasn't even sure that Jack would want to see her once he was settled since she was basically responsible for putting him here.

Finally a nurse entered. "You can go into Mr. Frost's room now."

Merry jumped to her feet. "How is he?"

"We've made him as comfortable as we can, and his temperature is down a little. He looks exhausted, so if you want to speak with him, you should go now."

Quickly Merry gathered her purse and jacket.

"Hey," she said as she stood over Jack's bed. He was frightfully pale and very still.

His eyes opened slowly. "Hey, yourself."

His voice was scratchy and his smile wan, but she felt a flicker of relief. He was important to her, she realized, although it was difficult to explain why she felt such attraction to this man who'd managed to criticize much of what she held dear.

"Is there anything I can do?" She felt helpless and surprisingly upset.

"Can you stay?"

"Here?" That was the last thing she'd expected him to ask. "With you?"

"Just for a while. I hate hospitals."

"Sure. I'd be happy to." She pulled a chair next to the side of the bed and sat down. Merry was not only taken aback at his request but curious as to what was behind it. Maybe nothing. Maybe he just wasn't crazy about being alone right how. She didn't doubt she'd feel the same.

"Jack, when was the last time you were in the hospital?" Pain flickered in his eyes. "When Jamie died."

"No wonder you don't like them. Don't worry, I'll stay as long as you want."

He nodded as his eyes drifted shut. In moments, he was asleep.

When she was sure he wouldn't wake, Merry slipped into the hall outside his door and called Abby.

"What's going on?" Abby demanded. Merry hadn't explained her absence beyond "Jack is sick."

"I'm in the hospital. They just admitted Jack. He's very ill. Double pneumonia, they think. I don't know what else."

"That's awful!"

"I'm going to hang around for a while. I want to talk

to the doctor. In fact, would you open the store tomorrow too? Things are so up in the air."

"Don't worry about it. In fact, I'll ask Hildy if she'll come over and help me. She can wrap gifts and keep the coffee and cookies going. That would help me a lot. You take the day off. Rest, if nothing else."

"You are the best, my friend. Thanks so much."

"What are friends for but to help in time of need? Take care of yourself, hon. I've got to go. There's a three-hundred-dollar sale heading toward the till right now."

Merry stepped back into the hospital room where Jack was sleeping and sat down beside him. As she looked at him, she wondered who it was she should call to inform them of his illness. He'd said he had a couple cousins, but what could they do if they had young children at home? She'd have to wait until he woke up to ask him. In a worst-case scenario, she could call his work. A man as handsome as Jack surely had a girlfriend who'd be worrying about him.

And if she were going to stay for a while, she wanted to be comfortable—or at least as comfortable as possible in a hospital room. She arranged the recliner and one other chair as best she could in order to stretch out, then leaned back to try to get some rest.

Perhaps she'd close her eyes for just a moment. . . .

Chapter Thirteen

....

"Miss? Miss?"

Someone was shaking her shoulder as Merry swam up from a deep sleep. "Hmmm?"

"Would you like a tray?"

Her eyes popped open. "Is it lunchtime?" She tried to straighten, but it was as if her muscles had molded to the chair.

Jack was still sleeping. His tousled dark hair, unnaturally rosy cheeks, and dry lips, slightly parted, were appealing, like those of a small boy sleeping. His vulnerability did something odd to Merry's insides.

"Not lunch. Dinner. It's roast chicken. Would you like some?" The aide held out a tray. Merry's stomach turned at the sight of milk and juice in paper cartons. The institutional covers over the plastic plates and the tiny packets of salt and pepper didn't bode well in her mind, but she nodded anyway. She'd slept away the day and her stomach was growling.

Next, the aide shook Jack by the shoulders. He winced and groaned, as if the touch hurt him.

"Why don't you come back in ten minutes with his tray?" Merry suggested. "If you can keep it warm till then, I'll wake him up and help him."

The aide looked relieved. "That would be great. The hospital is very full. There's a nasty bug going around, and our numbers are up."

Nasty bug indeed, Merry thought as she ate the pale piece of chicken and a baked potato. Both foods were the same color, and she wondered if boiled chicken wouldn't have been a better description. The squash was colorful but watery. Still, it tasted wonderful to someone as hungry as she.

How on earth had she slept so long? She'd have to chalk it up to exhaustion. Nights had been short and days long all month. She set aside her tray when the aide returned with Jack's dinner. Quietly she removed Merry's empty tray and left again. Merry hated to wake Jack, but he needed nourishment as well.

"Jack? Can you hear me? Can you wake up for dinner?" She put the tips of her fingers on his cheek and felt the unnatural heat there.

"Not hungry," he muttered.

"I'm not sure that matters. You haven't eaten. If you don't, the doctor will put you on a feeding tube, and I'm sure you don't want that."

The bedclothes stirred, and he opened his eyes. "I want to go home." He stared at her with a dark intensity that belied his condition.

"Home?" she echoed. "To California? Do you realize how long a trip that is?"

"Not there. Your place. I can sleep just as well there." He punched weakly at his pillow before closing his eyes.

So now he considered her place home?

She tinkered with the salt and pepper packets on his tray before she said, "You can talk to the doctor about that when he comes by. If you aren't eating, I'm sure he won't consider releasing you."

Not that he would anyway, Merry thought, but at least it got Jack struggling to sit up in bed.

He wasn't doing a good job on his own, so Merry pressed the bed's control button and, with her arm around his back, helped him up. She could feel him trembling and realized what a toll this had taken on him already. Sick or not, Jack was big, strong, and masculine, and it felt right to be holding him. Merry felt herself reluctant to let go.

Surprised at herself, Merry steadied him and left him to sit on his own. She didn't understand why Jack elicited this feeling within her. Jeff didn't. Zeke hadn't. The cute but persistent telephone man, Kip, didn't. She'd even disliked Jack when she'd met him. What was going on?

With every bite he took, Jack made a face, as if she were feeding him something awful. "This isn't as good as your food," he finally said.

"I'm so glad!"

He looked at her questioningly.

"I cook small portions for me and my B-and-B guests. I don't have to feed a building full of people. Considering the task, I think they do pretty well."

"Hmm . . ." He looked at her with unfocused eyes that slowly drifted shut.

His head lolled, and she could see him slipping off to sleep again. Merry eased his bedside table away, helped him find a more comfortable position on the pillow, and sat down to keep watch over him. She really should go home and tend to business, but she just couldn't leave. The man was sick, and there were no family or friends to look after him. And she really didn't mind. Asleep—and not bashing Christmas—was how she liked Jack Frost best.

* * * * *

Why was everyone trying to wake him up? Jack thought irritably as the voices in the room grew louder. Couldn't a man sleep when he wanted to? And he felt so rotten . . . every muscle and bone in his body ached. Even his hair and his fingernails hurt.

His head was filled with little men wielding sledge-hammers and pounding stakes into the backs of his eyes. He heard a groan and realized he was the one making it. Maybe he'd been hit by a truck. A semi. With a full load. Of iron.

"Here he comes." This time it was a male voice that spoke. Jack opened his eyes a slit, long enough to see a white coat and the end of a stethoscope. "Good morning, Mr. Frost. Remember me? I'm Dr. Henderson."

Jack felt someone settle on the edge of his bed. When he opened his eyes he saw the doctor peering down at him and Merry hovering anxiously over his shoulder.

"Wha . . . happened?" he managed.

"Basically, you caught a bad bug and quickly developed pneumonia. You're dehydrated. You're getting IV fluids and antibiotics right now, and we're going to keep a close watch over you. This stuff can turn nasty."

"*Turn* nasty?" Merry blurted. "It's already nasty!"

The doctor nodded and checked Jack's chart. "I've ordered respiratory therapy, and we'll give him oxygen if he needs it. I'm going to start him on potassium, and I've also ordered frequent blood draws to watch his white blood count." He turned to Merry. "Are you his wife?"

"No . . ." She felt a blush spreading across her neck and cheeks. Little did he know!

The doctor turned to Jack, who, although his eyes were

closed, seemed to smile a little. "Is there anyone you'd want me to give information to should you be unable to answer for yourself?"

"She's okay," Jack said without opening his eyes.

"Very well." The physician closed the chart, nodded to Merry, and turned to leave.

When he was gone, Merry neared the bed. "Are you sure you want to do that? Is there someone I should call? Family or friends? I'm hardly qualified to . . ."

"No one." He shifted restlessly as if he couldn't find a comfortable spot. "Everyone I know is in California."

She wanted to press him, but he was obviously miserable. She'd try again later.

Unfortunately, later was a long time in coming. As the evening progressed, Jack's fever elevated and his already fitful sleep grew even more restless.

Merry became alarmed as the parade of nurses, phlebotomists, and x-ray technicians grew.

Her cell phone rang, and she slipped into the hall to answer it.

"Hi, it's Abby. What's going on?"

"He's really sick. *Really* sick. I don't know what to do."

"Come home and sleep, that's what. He's in the hospital. Besides, he's not your responsibility."

Merry hesitated. "That's not exactly true."

"What do you mean? He's a complete stranger!"

Merry turned away so the nurse coming down the hall couldn't hear her. "The doctor asked for a next of kin or someone to confer with if Jack couldn't."

"And Jack chose you?" Abby didn't try to keep the shock out of her voice.

"There wasn't exactly a roomful of options. I was there. He didn't have much choice."

"I suppose . . ." Abby's tone was doubtful. "What does it mean, exactly?"

"For the moment, it means I have to decide if I'm going to stay here tonight or not."

There was a pregnant pause on the far end of the line. "You're kidding, right?"

"He's really sick, Abby." She didn't admit a part of her *wanted* to stay. While a healthy Jack Frost had annoyed her, this Jack was in need of help.

"Go home! He's in good hands. You won't do anyone any good if you don't get some rest."

Still, Merry hung around awhile longer, until Jack's sleep grew less restless. Every few minutes she touched his forehead, her fingers brushing his damp curls. If he was such a complete stranger, why did she feel so protective?

* * * * *

The next day Merry went to the administration office at her school to see if a substitute teacher could step in for her until after the Christmas holidays.

"I don't like to ask this, but I'm so far behind this year . . ."

Her principal waved away her words. "You are an excellent teacher, Merry. Your classroom is always ahead of the others. Having a sub right now isn't going to slow them down. Besides, my wife was at your store last week and said it was great. I'll have to visit myself."

When Merry told her students that she wouldn't be back until the new year, the reaction was quite different.

"No!" was the chorus when Merry made her announcement to her students. Even talking about all the parties and festivities in the offing didn't help.

"Teacher . . ." At the end of the morning Merry felt a tug on her sweater. She turned to see Greta standing behind her.

"Yes?" Merry took in the washed-out sweatshirt and high-water jeans the child was wearing.

"Don't go."

"I'm glad you'll miss me, Greta, but I'm afraid I can't change my mind now." She bent her knees so she was eye level with the child. "It won't be for long."

"But I'll miss you!" Greta's lower lip trembled perilously.

Merry gathered the child in her arms. "Maybe you and your parents can come to Frost for the live Nativity. There'll be real donkeys, sheep, and goats." Actually there would also be a cow or two, some horses, dogs, and a ferret. It seemed like everyone who had a beloved pet wanted it showcased in the Nativity scene, and she'd never had the heart to turn them away—even though she very much doubted there were ferrets in the manger.

"Really? I can come?"

"Absolutely. Have your mom call me and I'll invite her."

Wordlessly Greta circled Merry's legs and hugged her tight. Then she turned and ran from the room.

Greta, Jack, Hildy . . . all people who'd appeared in her life in the recent past. God must have something in mind for her. She'd have to trust that.

Chapter Fourteen

....

By the time she got to the hospital, Merry was unaccountably nervous.

What was her part in this? she wondered as she made her way to Jack's room. Hopefully he'd had a good night and the worst was past.

That seemed unlikely when she walked into his room and saw that he was nearly as pale as the sheet beneath him. The lunch tray on the bedside table was untouched.

His eyes opened when she touched his shoulder.

"How was your night?" she asked, although she already had a good idea.

"Lousy. Can you get me out of here? They poke me with needles every few minutes."

"You must be a little better. You're complaining." She sat down next to the bed where he could see her without moving his head.

At that moment the doctor stepped into the room. "Good morning. I hear your night wasn't much fun, Mr. Frost."

"They're trying to kill me. No one will let me sleep."

"It should be better tonight. Your white blood count is dropping, which is good. We'll also do another x-ray to see if your lungs are clearing up. You were a pretty sick fellow when you got here. And that's not to say you aren't still sick."

"I need to get out of here," Jack said and burst into a fit of coughing.

"Right," the doctor responded in a tone heavy with sarcasm. "We'll talk about that as you improve."

After he'd gone, Merry pulled her chair closer to Jack. "You've got to give me a number, someone I can call. A friend? Or don't you have any . . ." Her voice trailed away. He'd closed off so many parts of his life because of his brother; maybe he'd put up shutters on the social part of his life as well.

"You can let Vince, my VP of operations, know, but he can't do anything about it. He's got important things to do."

"More important than seeing that his boss is alive and well? I don't think so." Merry was indignant now. Jack was not only hard on himself, but he kept others from helping him. "You need an attitude adjustment."

"About Christmas?"

"That too, but mostly about being such an—an . . . *island*! You want to stand alone and not take any help. It's not necessary. You can quit punishing yourself over your brother any time now. . . ." Merry immediately regretted her words and bit her lip. "I'm sorry. I had no right to say that."

Jack studied her. "You think?" he said finally. He didn't sound angry, just puzzled.

She stayed with him until evening. They spoke very little, but she could tell he drew some sort of comfort from her presence. When he dozed off, she left the hospital and drove home, her mind in a whirl. Jack Frost had managed to tip her world in an entirely new direction.

* * * * *

An island? Jack mulled that over as he rested against the pillow. Is that what he was?

The cell phone on his bedside table began to ring. Jack wasn't sure he was glad that he'd asked Merry to get it out of his trouser pocket. For one thing, he didn't have the strength to reach far enough to answer it.

With a sigh, he mustered enough energy to grab it. "Yeah?" He could hardly believe it but he was winded from the exertion.

"Jack, is that you?" Vince sounded worried. "What's wrong, buddy?"

"I landed in the hospital." Every word was an effort. It had taken all he had just to get the phone off the table. He was weak as a kitten.

"I'll get a plane out there."

"Don't."

"What are you going to do when you get out? You can't lie around in a hotel room till you get better."

"Why not?" Vince was giving him a headache . . . or at least worsening the headache he already had.

"That's right, you've been staying in that B-and-B. Surely you can't ask them to take care of you! Why did you give your proprietor my number if you didn't want me to come?"

Jack thought of Merry's concerned touch on his forehead and the gentle way she'd brushed back his damp hair and decided that there wouldn't be a better place to recuperate—if Merry would agree. That was a big "if."

"Gotta go, Vince. Getting tired."

"Wait! Wait! I need to know exactly where you're staying and—"

Jack cut the connection and turned off the phone. Vince would just have to wait.

* * * * *

Merry arrived at the hospital about eleven o'clock in a pair of jeans and an oversized sweatshirt. She wore very little makeup, and her hair was pulled back in a simple ponytail.

Jack thought he'd never seen anything so beautiful in his life.

"You look a little better today," she greeted him, "like you might actually make it."

"I wouldn't take bets quite yet, but I finally think it's a possibility."

"I called your friend Vince." Merry pulled up a chair and sat down beside the bed. "I took his number from your cell phone. He sounded very upset."

"He called me already. He wondered where I'd recuperate once I get out." Jack watched Merry closely for any hint of what she might think of this question.

"What did you tell him?" She fingered the hem of his blanket absently.

"Well, he thinks I won't be able to go back to the B-and-B. If I know Vince, he's ready to charter a plane and whisk me off to California." Jack shifted in the bed. His muscles had never been so sore. Nor had he ever ached so deeply.

"I told him that if the owner would let me, I'd prefer to be at the B-and-B rather than anywhere else." His eyes locked momentarily with hers, and then she looked away.

"You've been pretty sick. It may take you awhile to recover."

"The same amount of time here or in California, I suppose."

"True. But in California you probably have a lot of beautiful women who'd offer to bring you food and sit by your bedside."

She was scouting for information, Jack thought.

"My secretary would volunteer. She's pushing retirement age and has been nagging me for years to take care of myself. She'd just love gloating over me saying 'I told you so.'" He tilted his head appealingly, much as he had as a small child when he was begging for something he wasn't sure he could have. It had worked then, and he hoped it would work now.

"Don't make me feel all guilty with those beautiful dark eyes of yours!" Embarrassment registered on Merry's face. "I mean, don't . . . too hard to resist . . . oh, forget it! I'm just digging myself a deeper hole."

"I'll pay you two hundred dollars a day if you'll help me stay here instead of having Vince try to kidnap me."

She looked horrified at his offer. "Oh, I couldn't take your money."

"Why not? The pilot would, the plane company would, my housekeeper would. They'd cost much more, actually. You'd be doing me a favor if you accept it. In fact, I'll pay you three hundred!" He intentionally pleaded with those "beautiful" eyes of his. He could see her weakening.

He didn't want to go back to California. There was little more for him there than there was here. He'd made himself dispensable at work, and Vince was capable of handling anything that came up. In fact, lately he'd begun to feel that if he disappeared it would take anyone but Vince weeks to notice he was gone.

Of course, if he were honest, he'd started disappearing at the time of his brother's death. After the accident he'd talked less, avoiding situations where people might ask him questions or look at him with judgment in their eyes. As an adult, he'd become a hard-driving businessman because it focused his mind in constructive directions. Had he not done so, who knows what might have happened to him by now?

He didn't allow himself the luxury of romance. Jamie never got a chance to fall in love so Jack wouldn't either was his circuitous, tortured thinking. It didn't matter that none of it made sense. It was simply another way of punishing himself for what had happened.

Merry studied his face so long that he began to grow uncomfortable.

What was she thinking behind those big green eyes? There was a sharp brain under those fluffy blonde curls. He began to wonder if he'd pressed his luck too far. Why on earth would she accept a stranger into her home and agree to play nursemaid? Jack lay back and closed his eyes. Another misjudgment on his part.

"You wouldn't go and die on me, would you? You've nearly scared the liver out of me more than once already."

Jack opened his eyes and saw that Merry was serious.

"Not if I can help it," he said, smiling faintly. "Thanks for your concern." She was actually thinking about it!

"I'd need to talk to the doctor first."

"Talk to me about what?"

Jack looked up to see his physician entering the room, chart in hand.

"If I take him back to my bed-and-breakfast, he's not going to suddenly get worse again, is he? I need to be sure he isn't going to scare me again."

The doctor chuckled. "There are no guarantees, but it's doubtful. We've found the right medications, and before he got sick he was basically a very healthy specimen. Besides, I would like him to give himself a few days before he travels anywhere."

She turned to Jack. "And you promise to listen to me and do as I say?"

"Without a doubt." He was going to have trouble with that one. He hoped he looked sincere and innocent.

"Well, okay then," she said, sounding resolved but not overjoyed. "There are only a few days until Christmas, and I have so much to do that it will be better to have him under my roof than for me to keep driving to the hospital. The living Nativity, the lutefisk supper, the Parade of Lights, gifts to wrap, food to cook, last-minute shoppers . . ." She sighed and eyed Jack speculatively. "Oh yes, and you are not going to pay me a ridiculous amount of money. If you feel well enough, you can work it off. I'm going to have you wrap gifts, like it or not."

Jack suppressed a smile and reminded himself not to get *that* well until after the holiday was over.

* * * * *

Merry ran into Zeke in the hallway as she was leaving Jack's room. He was scowling at her with a ferocity she'd never seen before.

"Is something wrong?" she asked, concerned about her friend.

"You're still here?"

"Where should I be?"

"At your store, for one." His voice was tight and controlled.

"Hildy and Abby are doing an amazing job there. We've already taken in much more than we did last year at this time." She frowned, perplexed at his behavior. "And why should you be worried about where I am every hour of the day?"

He looked exasperated. "Because you're my friend and I worry about you, that's why! I should never have steered Jack Frost toward your B-and-B."

"What does that have to do with anything?"

"He was only supposed to stay a couple nights, not move in permanently!"

The light dawned. "Are you jealous of Jack? Is that why you're upset?"

Zeke shifted awkwardly from one foot to the other.

"That's it, isn't it?" Merry was dumbfounded. She and Zeke hadn't dated for years, and yet here he was acting like a betrayed lover!

"Of course not," he said sternly before adding, "well, maybe a little." His cheeks reddened. "I can't figure out why you care this much. After all, he's none of your business!"

Merry put a hand to his mouth to silence him. Horrified, she suddenly realized that Jack could have overheard everything Zeke said.

Please, she petitioned silently. *I don't know what's going on, Lord, but don't let it get more complicated than it already is!*

Chapter Fifteen

Merry was steaming as much as her kettle when she brewed tea.

What business was it of Zeke's if she befriended Jack? She grabbed a mug from the cupboard and slapped it on the counter so hard that she had to check to see if it had cracked. She had no idea what was compelling Zeke to make a pest of himself right now, but it made her uncharacteristically angry. She didn't understand her own feelings any more than she did Zeke's.

There was a knock on the door. Jeff stood in the entry. She hadn't seen him since the night of the sleigh ride, but he looked as rugged and outdoorsy as ever and smelled of fresh air, pine, and horses.

"Hey, kiddo," he greeted her and gave her a bear hug.

"Hey, yourself." She slipped from his embrace to reach for another mug. "Tea?"

"Only if there are cookies with it. I'm more of a java

guy myself."

Cookies were never a problem at this house, Merry thought, especially at Christmas. She piled a plate high with her most recent baking efforts.

Jeff settled back in the chair looking comfortable in her cozy white kitchen. He seemed remarkably at home. But, she realized, he wasn't the man whose boots she wanted to permanently put beneath her table.

Merry could tell that Jeff was ready to plant himself there for a while, so she was relieved when Abby raced in, her eyes frantic.

"Can you come out to the store? It's crazy and I can't keep up."

"Be there in a minute." She turned to her guest. "Sorry, but I have to go."

Jeff rose reluctantly. "Sometime we need to be together when we aren't surrounded by people, Merry. I'd like to spend more time with you."

"It doesn't look like it will be anytime soon, Jeff." He reached for her, but she ducked out of his embrace. "So sorry . . ."

She escaped through the door to the shop and sagged against the shop wall, feeling she'd just escaped an embarrassing situation. Jeff wanted them to become a couple, and that was a conversation she wasn't ready to have.

Thankfully she was swept up in the bustle in the shop

and could push the issue to the back of her mind to be revisited another day.

That worked for an hour or two until her cell phone began to ring.

"Merry Christmas! Can I help you?"

"Hey, Merry, it's me," a male voice said.

"Who?" The voice wasn't even familiar to her.

"This is Kip . . . the phone guy. Remember me?"

"Of course." He was difficult to forget, despite the fact that she barely knew him.

"I've got a couple tickets for a basketball game at the Target Center tomorrow night. I was just wondering if . . ."

"That's very sweet, Kip, but I can't. This is the week before Christmas, and I keep the store open nights as well until Christmas Eve."

"Oh."

She could hear his disappointment, but she couldn't even let him down easy by promising to go out with him later. She simply wasn't sure she wanted to. What was happening today? Men were popping up all over the place—and she was turning them down.

All she could think about was Jack Frost!

* * * * *

Jack looked as white as the frost his namesake was purported to create, Merry thought as she helped him into his coat before they left the hospital. He'd lost a few pounds too. His clothing hung loose, and he'd quit combing the curls out of his hair so a dark forelock tumbled over his forehead. He looked unguarded and not completely in charge. Merry found the change oddly appealing.

He didn't complain as he slid into the front seat of her car, although she knew that he must ache all over. Instead, he closed his eyes, leaned his head back on the headrest, and sighed. She could see the tension and the effort that he was exerting simply to sit in the passenger seat.

"Now I know what 'weak as a kitten' means," she commented, keeping her voice light. "I remember Eggnog when I adopted him. He was so tiny, having lost his mother too early. You don't look much stronger than he was then."

Jack's eyes remained closed, but the corners of his lips tipped into a faint smile.

He seemed to doze as she drove toward Frost. Merry was anxious to get him home and settled before noon. Abby had a clinic appointment she couldn't miss, which left only Hildy to mind the store until Merry was free to help her. She was beginning to regret volunteering to be nursemaid. What had she been thinking? It was almost Christmas and she had yet to find a Joseph for the living Nativity, do last-minute errands for the Parade of Lights, and bake *lefse* for the lutefisk dinner.

Well, Jack would just have to entertain himself while he recuperated. She certainly wouldn't be able to wait on him hand and foot!

The house smelled of pine and peppermint when they entered. She'd received a new shipment of merchandise yesterday, and the partially unpacked boxes made walking difficult. Merry found herself hanging protectively onto Jack's arm.

He took the stairs to the second floor slowly and gave a sigh of relief as he entered his room. The fireplace was on and Merry had put a pitcher of ice water on the bedside table. "That was the longest trip I've taken in some time," he joked. "Man, am I weak." He dropped heavily onto the bed.

"You need something other than hospital food to build you up. I've got clam chowder and a protein smoothie for you downstairs."

"Smoothies?" His face wrinkled in disgust. "What's it made out of? Kelp and spinach? I don't eat that healthy stuff."

"You do here," Merry said calmly. "It's what you're paying me for."

"You should pay *me* to drink that stuff." He lay down on the bed and sighed. "Oh, man, this feels good."

"Do you want to eat now, or should I finish unpacking my new shipment first?"

It was a moot question, however, because Jack was

already fast asleep.

He did nothing *but* eat and sleep for the next two days. Merry was grateful because she got time to call the people participating in the Parade of Lights—mostly farmers who decorated farm equipment in the most amazing ways— and to round up a couple more entries. But she still had no one to play Joseph.

On the third day, Jack's eyes were clear and rested, and he was sitting up in bed reading from a pile of papers he'd copied at the courthouse.

"Feeling better, I see." Merry put a breakfast tray down on the bed.

"I was, until I started reading this stuff." He threw the papers onto the bed.

"Bad news?" She opened the curtains wide and let the sunshine in.

"Not for me but for several others in this area. How am I going to tell people to get off land they've thought was theirs? And the farmsteads . . ."

Merry looked up sharply. "You mean their *homes*? You own their homes as well?"

"Of course I do. It was all my great-grandfather's property."

"You can't kick people out of their homes," Merry blurted. When she saw the look on Jack's face, she bit her tongue. "I'm sorry. I know this isn't your fault. I'm just imagining what I'd feel like if someone made me leave this place. After all the hard work I've invested in it . . ." She shuddered. "It breaks my heart."

"You're a lot of help," Jack growled. "Now I feel even worse, but it has to be done. This mess has gone on too long. I can't leave it for another generation. My cousins' kids will have even less idea of what to do than I."

"Your cousins' children? What about *your* children?" She uncovered the plate on the tray, revealing fluffy scrambled eggs and thick slices of bacon.

"I don't have any, if you haven't noticed." He sounded touchy as he took the plate and dug into the scrambled eggs with a fork.

"Not now, but you might later."

"Doubtful." He picked up a piece of bacon and bit into it.

"Why not?"

"Fine father I'd be." His expression grew bleak. "Nobody would leave me alone with my own children for fear I'd do something stupid and hurt them."

"Nonsense! That's just some leftover lie from when you were twelve." Merry fidgeted with her hands before continuing. "I don't expect you to get over the loss of your brother, but you aren't the same person you were back then. Now you're a sensible, cautious, conscientious adult. Quit playing the tape of that child inside your head."

This wasn't the time to be having this conversation,

Merry knew. Fortunately at that moment Peppy entered the room at full speed chasing the cat, leaving neither of them time to say something they might regret. Nog shot onto the bed and into Jack's lap, his tail a big fur bottle-brush of distress. Peppy slid to a halt at the bed. From the safety of Jack's arms, the cat hissed and spat at his nemesis.

"What's gotten into you two?" Merry demanded. "You both know better than that."

As if the animal duo knew exactly what she was saying, they both deflated, their aggression fading away.

She turned to the cat. "Nog, what's so special about that guy? You don't like men!"

Jack scratched the cat behind the ears and a deep purr roared from its innards. "Could have fooled me."

"He's disliked every man who has walked through my door until now."

"Maybe Nog knows something you don't."

She wasn't sure she liked the smug way Jack smiled as he said it.

* * * * *

That evening, Merry knocked on Jack's door, a dinner tray in her hands. When she entered, she found him scowling first at the remote and then at the television.

She set down the tray and asked, "What's wrong? Does

it need new batteries?"

"No. New programming. Where are all the channels?"

"I don't have cable. You'll have to be happy with whatever you can find."

"You live out here in no-man's-land and you can't even watch television? What kind of life is that?"

"A pretty good one. There's no use paying for something I don't use. If you eat your meal"—she unveiled a medium rare rib eye and baked potatoes—"I'll play a game of Scrabble with you later."

He looked interested. "Promise?"

"Scout's honor. Now eat."

Merry hummed as she cleaned the kitchen. It felt domestic, homey . . . wifelike. She stopped cold, a sponge in her hand and a horrified expression on her features. She could say in all honesty that the thought had never entered her mind before this moment. Why now, with the man who could turn the town she loved upside down?

She filled a water glass and drank it quickly. She was tired, burning the candle at both ends with the store, the holiday plans, and running to the hospital. It was no wonder she couldn't think straight! A little rest and silly thoughts like that would be history, she assured herself.

She grabbed two pieces of apple pie from the counter

and headed for the stairs, determined not to let her mind drift in that direction again.

He was waiting for her, sitting in one of the two wing chairs. He'd pulled a small side table forward. "I have to let you know, I'm an excellent Scrabble player. I know every word that can be spelled with an *X* and a *Y*, and I go for the triple word counts."

She poured coffee from a carafe and took the game from a shelf. "And I can use all the letters at one time. Big scores. Huge."

"Sounds like we're perfectly matched."

She almost blurted, "A match made in heaven," but stopped herself. Wifelike, a match made in heaven . . . This domesticity was taking on a whole new feel and it was making Merry very uncomfortable.

* * * * *

They were perfectly matched, Jack realized—for every brilliant word he spelled, she responded with an equally stellar one. When the letters were all used, they were in a dead tie.

"Now what?" Merry asked as they stared at the board. "I've never had this happen before. I always win."

"You finally met your match." Jack grinned wickedly, some of the sparkle back in his eyes.

Your match . . . He was her match and she was his—

his perfect match. Luckily, Jack didn't have to pursue the concept further because his cell phone rang. A glance at the screen told him it was Vince.

"Hi, what's up?"

"You sound better. How are you feeling?"

"Okay. I'm at the B-and-B." Jack mouthed "Vince" to Merry.

"Perfect timing. I'll be there as soon as I can, but I have to finish a few things in the office first."

"You don't need to . . ."

"Don't try to talk me out of it. I have a lot of things for you to sign, for one thing. For another, I want to see where you stand in the business you're trying to get straightened out in Frost. And the third thing I want is to see you for myself. Merry said you've been very ill."

"You've been talking to Merry?" Jack was surprised he felt annoyed.

"I couldn't talk to you. Who else was there?"

"I suppose you're right." He still wasn't himself, Jack reasoned. Merry was the logical one to speak for him—except that it made everything seem too intimate. Jack Frost didn't let anyone get too close.

"Now may I talk to her?"

"What about?"

"It's my business, buddy. Is she there? Give the phone

to her for a minute."

Merry took the phone and said hello. She was silent then, listening to Vince. Her only words were "no problem" and "good-bye" before she handed the phone back to Jack. "He hung up. He says he'll see you soon."

"What did he want from you?"

"A room. He'll be staying here while he's in town."

Jack scowled. "Now both of you will be nagging at me."

Merry smiled at him sweetly. "Lucky you. Good night, Jack."

He stared at the door for a long time after she closed it. What was it about her that attracted him so? She was beautiful, of course, but it was her generosity, her guilelessness, and her intensity that piqued his interest. He'd never met anyone quite like her before. Of course there was the problem of their vastly differing views on Christmas, but surely that could be resolved—couldn't it?

He needed to get well, finish his business, and return to California as soon as possible. That was all there was to it. Merry was muddling his thinking and driving him crazy with this Christmas obsession of hers.

He looked at the pills she'd left for him. Quickly he put them in his mouth and swilled them down. He had to get out of here—and the sooner the better.

Chapter Sixteen

Hildy's footsteps were heavy on the stairs as she followed Merry up to Jack's room.

She seemed older lately, Merry had noted, as if the world's worries were piling up on her shoulders. Merry wished there was something she could do for the woman other than make sure she spent Christmas at her house. That would have to do for now, however.

It was going to be fun for Merry. She'd have Hildy, Jack, and possibly Vince under her roof. Maybe she'd invite Greta and her family too. Jeff and Zeke would no doubt want to be invited, but she would pass on that this year. Adding Jack and the unknown Vince to the mix might be too much testosterone under one roof.

She knocked on Jack's door and heard a muttered, "Come in."

He was doing the *New York Times* crossword puzzle and doing it faster than Merry had ever managed.

"Why don't you slow down with those things? If you finish them too quickly I'll run out of puzzles for you."

"I'm not good with tedium. This monotony is getting the best of me."

Jack hadn't bothered to comb his hair, and he was wearing a snug white T-shirt and navy sweat pants. His feet were bare. He looked youthful, rumpled, and adorable. Her fingers itched to brush back that tousled hair with her fingers. . . .

Quickly slapping that idea back into place, she stepped aside to reveal Hildy with her plate of lefse. "You've got company."

He brightened and looked very much like a little boy who'd gotten a reprieve from a well-deserved punishment. "Boy, Hildy, am I glad to see you."

"It can't be because of the poor food," the woman said wryly. "I think you've gained a pound or two since you came home from the hospital."

"Three. I weighed myself."

"But you lost eight," Merry reminded him. "What Hildy brought will help with that."

Hildy neared the bed and, with a flourish, unveiled a plate of lefse. It was similar in color to a tortilla, pale with brown spots left by the griddle. Each piece was rolled into a tight tube.

"I buttered them and put sugar on them for you." She thrust the plate into his hands.

"I've heard of lefse but don't think I've ever had it." He picked one up and smelled it.

"Just bite into it," Hildy ordered. "That's the only way you'll find out how it tastes."

Reluctantly he did so. As he chewed, a smile spread over his features. "This is good!"

"Of course it is," Hildy snorted. "I'm known for my lefse."

"What is it, exactly?

"It's soft Norwegian flatbread made with potatoes. Scandinavian tortillas, if you will."

Jack nodded and continued to eat.

Merry poured him a cup of coffee from the carafe on the table, and the two women watched him in amazement as he downed the entire plateful.

When he was done, he sat back against the pillows and sighed. "Thanks, Hildy."

"Thank *you*," she said with a chuckle. "I've never seen anyone enjoy my baking so much." She turned and eyed Merry. "It's good to have a man around the house to feed."

Hint, hint, Merry deduced, but she wasn't taking Hildy's advice. As soon as Jack was ready, she was packing him onto a plane headed for California.

Merry turned and saw Jack sprawled on top of the covers and out like a light. The food had put him to sleep. She sighed as she tossed a lightweight blanket over him and tiptoed toward the door with Hildy. She really didn't want to leave him, but while he was sleeping, she needed to get things done.

"Can you help out at the store for the rest of the week, Hildy? You've been a lifesaver for me."

"No problem. I don't have anything else to do."

Merry grasped Hildy's roughened hands in her own. "I'm planning on your being at my house for Christmas Eve and Christmas Day. You're still coming, aren't you?"

"I don't know why you bother with an old woman like me." Hildy looked incredibly sad as she said it.

"It's going to be interesting this year," Merry continued brightly. "I'm going to need you to help me. Jack and perhaps his friend Vince are going to be here as well. I thought I might also invite a family I met recently. They have a little girl in my class."

"A child?" Hildy looked interested now.

"I'm counting on you to be here." Merry gave Hildy a hug.

Hildy chuckled, a sound Merry didn't often hear from her neighbor. "You talked me into it."

* * * * *

Creaking from the upstairs floorboards signaled that Merry's patient was awake and restless.

She walked to Jack's door, which was ajar, and peered inside. Her rocking chair was sitting upside down, seat and back pillows on the floor and the rockers removed. He was kneeling on one knee examining the wooden joints of the chair.

"What are you doing with my mother's rocking chair? Have you broken it?" She tried to keep the horror out of her voice.

"Not breaking, fixing. This chair has been squeaking since I arrived. It needs to be re-glued."

"What's possessed you to fix it now?"

"I don't dare go downstairs because I'll be accosted by shopping women and motion-activated Santas. I've read every book on your shelves and put together a one-thousand-piece puzzle. It's time to get up and do something constructive."

"Jack, you may not admit it, but you've been very ill. It's good for you to rest."

"If I die of boredom it won't matter that I rest." He touched the rocker. "Do you have any wood glue?"

"I might, in the basement," she said in exasperation. "If I get it for you, will you quit trying to fix things?"

"Not unless you find me something else to do, something on your 'approved' list of activities." He grinned at her, a real, wide, enticing grin.

It was the first time she'd seen him so relaxed and so natural. He finally wasn't holding back. He was beginning to trust her. She knew trust was in short supply in Jack's world.

He obviously didn't trust even himself most of the time.

"I'll find something if you promise to behave until the doctor gives you the go-ahead that you're able to resume normal activities."

He grinned even wider. It did something incredible to his eyes. They fairly danced with good humor. "You mean I can misbehave after that?"

"You are incorrigible!" She couldn't help but return the smile. "I'll be back as soon as I get time, and I'll bring a project for you."

"No cleaning the silver service or folding clothes," he warned. "Something interesting."

"Would I fail you?" she retorted.

Suddenly he grew very still and his eyes serious. "No, Merry, I don't believe you would."

* * * * *

"We're out of replacement bulbs for the lights on the Christmas trees," Abby informed her when Merry returned to the store. "And we only have one set of silver reindeer left. Besides that, there's been a run on tablecloths."

The hum of happy conversation surrounded them as customers picked up last-minute Christmas gifts.

"There are more lights in the storage closet. I accidentally labeled them 'ornament hangers.'"

"Of course." Abby sighed dramatically. "That makes perfect sense." She was beginning to show the wear and tear of the season. Her eyes were weary and her perkiness somewhat subdued.

"Hang on, Abby," Merry encouraged. "It isn't long until Christmas now. That reminds me, when we sell out of tablecloths, offer them table runners and placemats. It's too late to order more."

In fact, Merry observed, her little store was slowly emptying. There were gaps where trees once sat, and most of the ornaments left on the shelves were purple or teal. She'd decorate a tree with those for the after-Christmas sale. They'd sell immediately then.

The cell phone in her pocket rang. When she answered, it was Vince's voice on the other end of the line.

"Hi, Merry. Vince here. I just landed in Minneapolis. I'm standing in line to get my rental car. Would you give me directions to your place? It's not showing up on my GPS."

"Here already?" She hadn't even checked his room yet to see that it was ready for a guest. And she didn't have time to bake fresh cookies for him like she usually did for guests. Oh well, Vince didn't sound like the kind of guy who'd mind too much.

When she hung up, she petitioned, *Lord, make this all work out. I don't know the whys of all that's going on, but I know You are in charge. Help Jack to finally heal both physically and emotionally and me to know what I can do for him and his friend. And Greta, I pray for her family . . . and Hildy . . . and . . .* She could have gone on all day, she realized. Fortunately God already knew what everyone needed and was able to accomplish without her help if He so chose.

"Merry?" Abby shook her by the sleeve. "Why are you just standing there in a daze?"

She blinked. "I almost forgot. I have to find a project that will entertain Jack Frost."

"That won't be easy," Abby commented, "unless you give him windowpanes and brushes and ice to frost them with."

Something clicked in Merry's head. "Abby, you are absolutely brilliant. That's what I'll do!"

She left Abby standing dumbfounded and headed for the kitchen. She knew now what entertainment she could provide for Jack.

* * * * *

A short time later, Merry entered his room carrying a fishing tackle box, a thick pad of paper, and an easel.

"What's this?" Jack sat up on the bed. He'd felt a little woozy from fiddling with the chair and had retreated to the bed to rest as soon as Merry had left. Maybe he wasn't quite as strong as he thought he was. Of course, he'd never admit that to Merry.

"Something to entertain you."

"I'm going fishing? Is that on the doctor's list?" He stared at the tackle box.

"Don't be silly." She put the box and paper on the table and set up the easel beside the window. She put the pad of watercolor paper on it and opened the tackle box with a flourish.

"Paints?" He stared into the box of brushes and tubes of color.

"Watercolors. You'll enjoy them." She told him what Abby had said about Jack Frost and windows.

"What do you expect me to do?" He stared at the equipment like it was crawling with vipers. "I haven't held a brush in my hand for years."

"I expect you to stay out of my hair and to paint quietly until dinnertime."

"That's hours. I could paint the Sistine Chapel by then—if I really knew how to paint."

"Have at it. By the way, Vince called. He's in the Twin Cities. He'll be here in a couple hours. You'd better get busy." She ran water into a tin container and set it on the bedside table. "Have fun."

Fun. So this was Merry's idea of fun. Her personal life was even more mind numbing than his. Jack stared at the paper for a long while before picking up a pencil and, in faint sketches, imagining what the fictional Jack Frost might create. There was a brief moment in time when he'd entertained the idea of being an artist. *Frost Brothers Gallery* was the name he'd imagined. But Jamie was more gifted in that area, so Jack had backed off even before he'd started.

He had no idea when he'd quit painting and fallen asleep, he realized as he heard Vince's familiar voice on the stairs. He barely had time to open his eyes before his friend burst into the room.

"So this is where you've been hiding out!" Vince took in the fireplace, the décor, and Jack's pale features. "Very smart. I like it. And Christmassy. I feel like I'm in Macy's in December." He strode across the room and sat down on the bed by Jack, who'd struggled to a sitting position. "You look horrible, buddy."

"Glad to see you too." Jack gave a weak grin.

"Miss Merry says you've been working too hard sorting out this land deal. She also says you're less than an ideal patient, that you're restless, bored, and itching to get back to work."

"True, true, and true," Jack admitted. "But now that you're here, you can do it in my place." Vince was the only person he'd trust with the task.

"Now that that's settled, how are you feeling?"

Jack took an internal scan of himself. He hadn't been feeling much of anything, but now that Vince was here to help, he could relax.

"Achy, weak, like my limbs aren't working together."

"Good thing I got here when I did."

At that moment Peppy and Nog came racing into the room, playing one of their chasing games. Nog leapt onto the bed and into Jack's arms. Peppy skidded to a stop at the foot of the bed and began to whine.

"Okay, you can come up here too," Jack said and the dog jumped onto the bed, his tail wagging wildly. The cat, meanwhile, had settled in Jack's arms and was purring loud as a Sherman tank.

Vince's jaw dropped. "I didn't think you liked animals."

"I do if they like me." Nog purred and put his nose under Jack's chin to nuzzle him.

"Well, I'll be . . . This is amazing."

"That's what Merry says too. She says her cat hates men."

At that moment, Nog seemed to realize Vince was there and hissed at him. Then he curled back into Jack's chest and began purring again.

"So I see." Vince glanced at Merry, who'd come in and stood by the easel near the window. "To what do you attribute this love relationship between your pets and Jack? I would have bet money they'd hate him."

"Me too," she responded absently. "I think he bribes them with treats."

"Do not." Jack patted Peppy's rump. "They love me for myself."

"Then they're the only ones who do," Vince joked. He stood up and walked toward Merry. "What are you looking at?"

"These watercolors. Jack, did you really do these?"

"Of course. It's not like I had the opportunity to hire outside help. What's wrong with them?"

Merry didn't take her eyes away from what Jack had created. "Nothing. Absolutely nothing. They're amazing!" She held one up for Vince. "Fernlike frost on a windowpane with the sun filtering through it. It looks so real."

"Isn't that what I, Jack Frost, am famous for?" Jack didn't take her seriously.

"Really, Jack, these are good."

"I may have taken a few art classes in my day, but never to rave reviews."

"I have to agree with her, buddy," Vince said. "I had no idea you had it in you."

Jack looked doubtfully at them. "Right."

Merry spun around. She was holding one of the frosty scenes. "May I sell this in my shop?"

"Are you crazy? These are simple little sketches, not artwork!"

"I know they are simple. That's part of their charm. You've caught the idea of a frosty morning in so few strokes. I have some beautiful frames that would be incredible with these. I think people would buy them for last-minute gifts. Wait, I'll show you." She took a picture frame off the bookshelf, popped out the photo of her parents, and demonstrated what Jack's picture would look like framed. "Nice, right?"

Vince and Jack stared at the result.

It did look good, Jack realized in amazement.

She gathered the paintings and thrust them at Jack. "You'll sign them, of course. Original paintings by the real Jack Frost!"

Vince thrust a pen into his hands and ordered, "Sign. These are great."

He was so accustomed to signing things for Vince that Jack didn't hesitate. It wasn't until later that Jack wondered why he'd been so willing to put his John Hancock on something so silly.

Chapter Seventeen

Vince settled down in a chair across from Jack and studied him until Jack scowled.

"What are you looking at?"

"You've lost a few pounds, but it looks good on you. How are you feeling?"

"You don't care about that. You know the answer. What's going on in that brain of yours?"

"Merry's a beautiful woman."

"I suppose," Jack said grudgingly. Merry was beautiful but Vince was irritating him.

"She's been taking good care of you."

"I haven't died, I guess."

"That's not as funny as you think, Jack. You were pretty close, according to Merry. She was very frightened for you. She might have saved your life. If you'd been in a hotel you never would have called an ambulance."

"I hadn't thought about that," Jack admitted, suddenly realizing that Vince was probably right.

"Why don't you marry her?"

"Where did that come from? We hardly know each other." Jack squirmed uncomfortably.

"She probably knows you better than ninety percent of the people who *think* they know you. It's time you let your guard down."

Jack laughed humorlessly. "Right. 'Oh, by the way, Merry. Thanks for putting me up at your B-and-B—and will you marry me?'"

"You could be a little smoother than that."

Vince was actually serious, Jack realized. He needed to change the subject, quickly.

"What we need to talk about right now is the mess at the courthouse. There was a trust set up through which the taxes were paid and no one questioned it. It had always been done that way and no one researched it further. Far as I can figure out, something was recorded incorrectly at the courthouse at that time. The proof is there that the land was never sold to them, but for all intents and purposes, they consider it theirs."

Vince shook his head somberly. "I'll look it over and run it by another attorney to make sure we have it sorted out before we say anything to anyone."

Jack closed his eyes and groaned.

"I'll take care of everything. You've done all the legwork. Your job is to get stronger now. Frankly, anything you try to do, I'll consider interference."

Jack was surprised that all he felt was relief.

"I'd also suggest you take my advice about Merry. She's awesome—businesswoman, entrepreneur, cook, teacher, and nurse. You don't run into that combination often. And she'd be good for you. She chooses joy while you are stuck in the sad history of your family. Merry's the best medicine for you. Don't think I don't see it, Jack."

"You need glasses," Jack muttered. Suddenly he was very, very tired.

After Vince left it was only moments before Jack fell asleep.

He was there, at the precipice, his hands on Jamie's shoulders as he sat on the sled. They were laughing.

"Push me, Jack, push!"

"It looks pretty high, Jamie. If Mom knew . . ."

"But she doesn't. Come on, Jack. You're always so serious. You don't know how to have fun."

"Do too." Jack felt a chill creep up his legs. The sun was bright but cold.

"Do not."

"Do too." But he said it doubtfully. Jamie was right. He wasn't the fun twin. He was the scholar—Jamie, the party. He drew a deep breath, and the icy air burned his lungs.

"Push!" Jamie yelled.

Jamie thought he was a coward. That was even worse than the scolding they were bound to get from their mother. Jack pushed.

Then Jamie lay crumpled at the bottom of the hill.

"Wake up! Wake up!" Merry's voice distracted him from the scene at the bottom of the hill. He swam slowly out of the nightmare, and Merry's concerned features came into focus. "It's okay. You were dreaming. I could hear you from down the hall."

Jack shuddered.

With a soothing hand, Merry stroked his forehead and made comforting, wordless sounds. He was sorry when she stopped.

"That must have been one horrible dream." Her pretty features were wrinkled with concern.

"Nothing I haven't had before." Jack struggled to sit up and took the glass of water she offered. "It's very infrequent now, not like when I was a kid."

"About your brother?"

"Yes. That day—it's all crystal clear and exactly as it happened."

"I'm so sorry." She put her hand over his. Her fingers were warm, strong, and comforting.

"No big deal." It was a big deal, of course, but he was glad she began to play the denial game with him.

"I came up to get those pictures you painted," she said cheerfully. "I need to put them in the shop."

"You were kidding about all that, right?"

"Not in the least." She picked up what she'd come for, smiled a heartbreakingly tender smile, and walked out of the room, leaving Jack more bemused than ever.

* * * * *

Merry carried Jack's paintings downstairs to the kitchen. Then she stole into the store and gathered up frames that might work with the scenes. She didn't tell Abby or Hildy, who'd come over to help wrap gift items, what she was doing.

She had just finished framing the last one when Abby entered the kitchen.

"I'm taking a quick break. It's quiet right now and Hildy's at the till." Abby plopped onto a stool. "My feet are killing me." She glanced at the table and the framed art spread across it. "What's this?"

"Something new for the store. Do you like it?"

Abby picked up one of the smaller pieces. "Gorgeous. It's as though you can look through the glass and see what's behind the frost." She squinted. "Look here. There's even glitter on the frost to reflect light. Someone with a lot of attention to detail did this."

Merry hadn't even noticed the sparkle before, but she did know there was a tube of silver glitter in her paint box. Jack hadn't missed a thing.

"That's cute." Abby giggled. "It's signed 'Jack Frost.' Fitting, I suppose, but why wouldn't the artist want his or her own name on something this beautiful?"

"It's a man who painted them, actually." Merry poured coffee for them and sat down at the table. "And his name *is* Jack Frost."

Abby's eyes grew wide, and she pointed her index finger to the ceiling. "That Jack Frost? The one upstairs? I didn't know he could paint!"

"Apparently he didn't either. I gave him my paint box to keep him busy and out of trouble, and he did these. Aren't they amazing?"

"You're going to sell them?" Abby couldn't draw her gaze away from the table.

"I thought I'd try. He thinks it's all crazy, but he obviously has no idea how good these are."

Abby jumped to her feet. "There's a lady in the store right now who might be interested. She said she wanted to give everyone in her family a piece of art this year. I've got to show her these!"

That left Merry at the table alone with her thoughts.

What was it about Jack that appealed to her so? Granted, he was rich, good-looking, and, when he wanted to be, charming. He could also be irascible, testy, and stubborn.

She leaned back in the chair and thought of him during those days at the hospital when he was vulnerable, his emotions exposed. The pain of his brother's accidental death had never left him, and he'd carried the heavy load so long. Merry wished she could carry some of that ache for him.

She sat up straight. The thought shocked her. Never before had she felt that way about someone. She was always willing to help, to champion, to comfort, but it wasn't in her nature to want to be so sacrificial—until now. Until Jack.

* * * * *

Hildy left early saying something about rising bread dough, but at closing time, Abby approached Merry with sparkling eyes. "You'll never believe it, Merry!"

Merry looked up absently. She'd been restocking shelves, visiting with customers, and trying to process her feelings for Jack. Now the customers were gone and the shelves stocked, but she was more confused than ever about her emotions. It had set her back on her heels, in fact.

Abby thrust out her hands. She was holding a large wad of bills. "This is what we made on Jack's paintings!"

"There has to be at least nine hundred dollars there . . . surely not . . ."

"People loved them. The smaller ones went first, but they were still asking for them after we ran out. I sold a couple of the bigger ones too."

"How did you know what to charge?"

"The first lady who came to the counter with one of the larger ones said she'd seen something like it at a gallery that was priced at three hundred dollars, so I said they were two hundred. She didn't even blink. In fact, she said she wanted to know more about the artist. Her husband is an art teacher at a high school, and they collect new artists' work."

Abby grinned at Merry's stunned expression. "So you'll have to get Jack to write up a little bio about himself and his experience that we can hand out with each piece that's purchased."

Merry's mouth worked but nothing came out. Surely this entire day was a dream, and she'd wake soon.

Then Vince loped downstairs while Jack followed him at a more sedate pace.

"Are they gone? The customers, I mean. Is it safe to come out?" Jack asked.

Merry nodded numbly, and Abby giggled. "I can't wait to hear how he reacts when you tell him. Gotta go now, though. Hubby said he'd take me out for dinner tonight."

"Tell me what?" Jack's gaze caught Merry's.

"What are you doing out of bed?"

"I'm not a child, Merry! I'm a grown man and if I feel like being here . . ." Jack swayed a little. "Right now I feel like sitting down."

"Take him in the kitchen, Vince," Merry suggested. "I've got pork chops in the oven. Maybe he'll be less dizzy with some food in his stomach."

"I hate it when you're right," Jack muttered to her.

She grinned and patted his arm. "Just wait till you hear what I was right about now."

She wouldn't tell the pair anything until she'd set the table, dished up the food, and said grace.

"Now will you tell me?" Jack demanded. "I've been ill. It's not healthy to keep me in suspense."

"Now you admit you've been sick? It's certainly taken you a long time!"

Vince grinned but said nothing. It was obvious he enjoyed the repartee.

"Those watercolors you did today?"

"What about them? You can just toss the bunch. I was trying to paint what I saw in my head, but they didn't come out quite like I wanted them to." Jack dug into a bowl of squash and grabbed the bit with a hunk of butter melting on top.

"After I framed them, Abby sold some of them. We made nine hundred dollars."

Jack's fork clattered to the table and Vince's jaw dropped in amazement.

"Nine hundred? For what?" Jack finally managed.

"For some lovely pictures of winter scenes." Merry watched him with amusement. Dumbfounded was the best way to describe him at the moment.

"But I just looked out the window and painted what I saw."

"You have amazing natural ability, Jack. Don't you know that?"

"How would I know? The last time I remember painting or drawing was in grade school. Before . . ." He closed his eyes for a moment and opened them again. "My brother, Jamie, was the one with the artistic talent. My parents were always raving about the things he drew. Far be it from me to rain on his parade, I guess. I was always better with numbers, so we each had our own skills."

"Good. I'm glad you're good at numbers." She reached into her pocket and pulled out a wad of money. "I'll tell you the cost of the frames I added, take ten percent commission, and the rest is yours."

Vince chuckled. "It sounds like you are well acquainted with math yourself. If I were you, I'd ask for at least twenty percent commission. After all, without you, this talent would have remained hidden forever."

Jack was still staring at the pile of bills. "This is crazy. You take the money, Merry."

"I certainly will not! I don't do business that way. Besides, now you'll have to paint more pictures for me. Do the smaller ones this time. I'm sure I can sell them all."

"What have I gotten myself into now?" Jack asked Vince.

"You've gotten yourself into very good hands, my friend, and also a new career. Tonight you can brief me on what you've been doing so far, and I'll take over from here. You don't look very well, for one thing, and for another, the demand for your paintings is obviously high and you need to strike when the iron is hot." He turned to Merry. "Don't you think so?"

"Absolutely." Merry was relieved that Vince would take some of the burden off Jack, who was not nearly as strong as he insisted he was.

"But you can't work tonight until after the Parade of Lights. I think we're going to have our best participation ever." She glanced at the clock on the wall. "Which reminds me, I'd better get going. I'm supposed to help the entries line up. You can watch from the front window. Just turn the rest of the lights off in the house so you can really see the parade well."

"I don't want to . . ." Jack began.

Vince lightly punched his shoulder. "But I do. You're going to watch this if I have to tie you up to get you to do it. I'm in Frost and I'm determined to enjoy it."

"Traitor," Jack muttered. "I thought you came here to help me."

"I did," Vince assured him. "Believe me, I did."

* * * * *

A hodgepodge of people and their parade entries greeted her at the edge of town.

Merry pulled a sheet of paper out of her pocket and walked up to a John Deere tractor outlined in small white lights. The driver was dressed in a Santa costume, but Merry still recognized him. "Hi, Doug, you are entry number three. Line up over there and leave room for two other tractors ahead of you."

Next sat a plow with a snow scoop full of elves. "Number four. Behind Doug," Merry called out.

A group of tiny carolers waited in a clump. "You kids will be last—except for the horses, of course—we don't want you stepping in anything . . ." Her voice trailed off. "So get ahead of the miniature horse and Jeff and his Percherons. He'll go slow or stop if you get behind."

And so it went until Merry had given everyone their position in line.

"Okay, folks, it's time to start. We'll go up and down every street in town. People are lined up on the street and in their cars. First entry can go. Everyone follow at a suitable pace. You know the rules. There will be cider and treats at the community center after and music by Frost's very own musical group, The Frosties."

Her job was done. Nearly everyone in the parade had done this before and it was old hat to them. She walked along the entries smiling at the pickup truck decorated to look like a gingerbread house and the "Santa car" that resembled a sleigh.

"Hey, Merry. Looking for a ride?"

Jeff had his favorite sleigh out tonight, the one he used

on special occasions. It was just right for two people. Merry imagined the original owners of this vehicle wrapped in warm furs and blankets, heating their feet with bricks wrapped in rags at the bottom of the sleigh.

"I said, are you looking for a ride?" Jeff called. "You can come with me. There are blankets to wrap up in."

Willingly she crawled aboard. He put his arm around her shoulders and gave her a squeeze.

* * * * *

"Are you sure about this?" Vince asked Jack as they made themselves comfortable on the front porch of Merry's house. "I think you should be inside."

"Fresh air is good for a person. Isn't that what everyone says? We're dressed properly for the weather. Besides, how are we going to see this parade Merry is so excited about if we have to stare through glass? We can't get the ambience of the event inside the house."

"Since when have you cared about ambience or mood or whatever? Don't blame me if you get sick again."

Vince was silent for a moment then added, "She's beautiful, you know. And kind. A really lovely woman."

"Yes, I've realized that."

"You aren't getting any younger, and it's time you had someone in your life besides me and the very few others you allow in. I've seen you smile more today than I have in the last six months."

"Is that so?" Jack hadn't realized that, but he knew he was happier here than he'd been in a long time—despite the legal hassles and his hospital stay. "To what do you attribute that?"

"Merry, of course. If you let her slip through your fingers, you're a fool."

"You talk like I even have her in my fingers. She's an independent woman who thinks for herself. And who says, other than you, I want someone in my life?"

"Don't kid me, Jack. You've punished yourself enough. Quit denying yourself the things you really want. It's not going to bring Jamie back."

Jack didn't speak. There was nothing to say. He didn't disagree with Vince, but he'd lived this way a long time. He'd grown accustomed to refusing himself. Some people resisted change, even in bad situations, because they were afraid of what the future might bring. That was him. Jamie's death had been the center of his existence. Without that, where would he be?

The first of the floats drove by the house. On a flatbed pulled by a tractor were several children sitting around a Christmas tree, gazing up into its branches. Christmas music played from inside the cab of the John Deere.

Two more tractors passed and then a fire truck polished to a glossy sheen. The fireman driving it and the Dalmatian hanging its head out the window both wore Santa hats.

And so it went—machinery, cars, trucks, the occasional flatbed, all playing carols and decorated for the season. Finally the children's chorus came by. Jack looked hard at the children and spotted little Greta walking along, looking proud and singing at the top of her lungs.

Jack stood up when he spied the miniature horses. "Time to go in. I'm getting cold."

"Don't you want to see Merry go by?" Vince asked as he pointed to Jeff's sleigh with the two of them perched high on the seat and sitting very close together.

Jack stopped and turned toward the street. There was Merry, in a red-and-white *Cat in the Hat* top hat, beside Jeff. She was rubbing her hands against the chill and talking animatedly. Then she saw the pair on her front porch and waved. Her smile lit the night as brightly as any of the parade lights.

Jack spun around and stomped inside.

As he followed, Vince said nothing, but Jack could feel his speculating gaze burning though his shirt.

"You don't like it much, do you? Seeing Merry with other men, I mean."

"It's a free country. She can be with anyone she chooses." Jack knew his tone was short but he couldn't help it.

"And you're comfortable with that?" Vince probed. "Wouldn't you rather just have her with you?"

Jack was suddenly furious. It wasn't because Vince was prying into his affairs but that what he'd said was true. He *would* like to have Merry all to himself—and she'd never let on that the feeling might be mutual.

He was relieved when the door opened and Greta ran inside.

"Miss Merry invited my family over for hot chocolate before we go to hear the music at the community center," she crowed. "Did you hear me sing?"

"Like a songbird." Jack didn't feel like smiling but he did so for the child.

"It was fun." Greta shed her jacket, boots, hat, and mittens before running to the chair in which Jack was seated and crawling into his lap. "Feel my cheeks. They are so cold!"

At that moment Greta's parents entered with Merry right behind them. To Jack's relief, no Jeff followed.

Merry also went directly to Jack. "You were outside. You should have stayed in."

"Fresh air and all that." He tried to be flippant, but the genuine concern in her eyes touched him.

"Just don't get sick again, that's all I ask." She turned toward the others. "Who's ready for cocoa?"

Chapter Eighteen

When Merry left for the kitchen, Greta and Vince followed her, leaving Stephanie and Wayne alone with Jack.

"Merry has been awesome," Stephanie commented. "She's been so generous including us in these Christmas events we otherwise wouldn't have had. And the pastor has offered help as well."

"No family? Either of you?" Jack could identify with that.

"I've been estranged from my family for years," Wayne admitted. "I didn't have the healthiest upbringing." Pain flickered in his eyes. "I don't want Greta to have a repeat of my childhood. That's why I've been so worried since I lost my job . . ."

"She has two sane and sober parents who love her!" Stephanie interrupted. "Don't forget that." Tears sprang to her eyes. "That's more than I'd hoped for."

Jack looked at her curiously.

"My first husband, Greta's father, passed away," Stephanie said. "When he did, I totally fell apart. I went into a deep, destructive depression. I didn't function at all for months and tried to hide from everyone and everything. I'm not sure what would have happened to me had it not been for Wayne." She reached out and touched his arm. "He was God-sent, I'm sure of it.

"I'd gone from being a loved, pampered wife to a heartsick, desperate woman in the blink of an eye. Meeting Wayne was the first flicker of hope I'd had in a long while."

"I wanted nothing more than to provide a good home for both my girls, and I had a pretty good job until the economy tanked." Wayne looked pensive. "But we'll make it. Somehow . . . we'll make it."

They all turned when they heard someone clear their throat.

"Sorry." Vince stood in the doorway between the living room and kitchen. "I didn't mean to eavesdrop, but Merry told me to come and get you. Food's ready."

"Sorry." Wayne jumped up and held out his hand to his wife. "We don't want to keep our hostess waiting. We still have to go to the community center to hear the music."

Vince lingered while Jack rose slowly from his chair.

"Tired?"

"I hate to admit it, but yes." Jack put his hand behind his neck and massaged it wearily. "I'm worthless these days. Merry keeps ordering me to rest, but there's so much to do."

"Leave it all to me. Pretend you're on a cruise ship heading somewhere without Wi-Fi or cell service. You're out of touch unless I say so, okay?"

"What if you do something I don't agree with?"

"Then you can fire me." Vince wasn't joking.

"I'd rather not, so don't do anything that will destroy families or ruin the family name."

"I just hope," Vince muttered, "that those two goals aren't mutually exclusive."

* * * * *

When Greta and family put on their coats, Merry was reluctant to see them leave. She'd grown deeply fond of this little family in the time she'd known them.

"Have you got plans for Christmas Eve?" Merry inquired.

"Not yet. I imagine we'll go to church somewhere," Stephanie said.

"Then you'll come here. Jack and Vince will be here, and my neighbor is coming over. I'd love to have a full table. Please?"

"Wouldn't that be a lot of extra work?"

"For a woman who loves the holidays? Hardly. The more the merrier."

Stephanie glanced up at Wayne. "Greta would love it."

Wayne grinned. "So would we."

"It's settled then. We'll eat at six. Come early for appetizers and games."

"Games?" Jack said weakly from across the room.

"Yes, games," Merry said firmly. "You'll have fun."

"Whether you like it or not," Vince added with a chuckle, obviously enjoying seeing his boss unable to compete with a force of nature like Merry.

"Our church lutefisk supper is coming up in a couple days," Merry said to the young couple. "It's the same night as our living Nativity. Please come to that too, if you can."

"What's lutefisk?" Wayne asked. "Sounds like a musical instrument."

"Codfish soaked in lye. That is how the Scandinavians preserved it. It's served with boiled potatoes, peas, and melted butter." Merry laughed out loud at the expression on Wayne's face. "It's better than it sounds. See you there?"

"If I come—and I won't promise—I'll bring antacids."

After they left, Merry turned to Jack and Vince. "Vince, you don't look so good."

"Codfish and lye? Do people really eat that?"

"The lye is rinsed away before you eat it." She smiled beneficently. "Granted, it may be an acquired taste, but I've learned to enjoy it."

"I've heard of it," Jack said, "but I don't think I've ever eaten it."

"I don't want to learn anything new," Vince muttered, "especially that."

Jack burst out laughing.

"What's so funny?" Vince growled.

"You're learning plenty, my friend, whether you like it or not. Merry has that effect on people."

After Merry excused herself to go to bed, Vince and Jack remained downstairs amid the twinkling lights and holiday ornaments.

They both stared into the fire, lost in their own thoughts.

Vince was the first to speak. "That little family's situation is pretty heart wrenching."

Jack nodded thoughtfully. "I've been living in an ivory tower. You hear about people who have lost everything but never really take it in—until you meet them. Is there anything we can do for them? Find them a house, a job, something." He'd always been generous with his money but usually left it to Vince to decide where the company's charitable contributions went.

"I'll do it, but I have other things to do first." Vince stretched lazily. "I have been looking at stuff at the courthouse. Your suspicions are correct. I've found serious errors in the recording of your property, including homes in town that are yours as well."

"Houses people are still living in?"

"I don't know yet, but if there's an empty one, there's no reason not to allow Stephanie and Wayne to live in it."

"Do your best." Jack yawned. "I just want this over."

"Then I have your permission to move ahead with everything?"

Jack rubbed a finger on the point between his eyes. "I'm too tired to hear any more tonight. I trust you."

"Good. I'll get things moving tomorrow."

* * * * *

"You're looking better today," Merry commented the next morning as she poured Jack a second cup of coffee. Vince, in a very professional looking shirt and tie, had eaten two hours earlier and headed out.

"I finally had a good night's sleep." Jack scraped his fingers through his hair, which left it tousled. "I told Vince to handle the business with the land around Frost. I don't want to worry about it anymore. I feel like I've been hit by a freight train and I might as well admit it. Is there anything you'd like me to do around here? I'm pretty handy with a hammer and nail and I've been known to change a lightbulb."

Merry studied him thoughtfully. "How are you at breaking down boxes? I've got an entire basement full of them from my orders."

"Consider it done."

"And I'm having trouble with several strings of lights . . ." It felt surprisingly good to have someone to help her with a to-do list.

"I'll take care of it."

"My microwave went on the fritz."

"I'll see what I can do."

They stopped for a break at noon. It was pleasant to have someone brew coffee and make her a sandwich when she had a moment to rest. Jack looked good in her kitchen.

"This is a stellar grilled cheese sandwich," Merry said as she savored a bite. "I think it must be the tomato slices that do it."

"My specialty. Wait until you taste my chicken salad sandwiches. And tuna fish . . ." He took a bite of his own sandwich and nodded approvingly.

"Do you ever eat anything besides sandwiches?"

"Soup. Lots of soup. Or I eat out."

"You are the clichéd bachelor. It doesn't sound like much fun. You'd be a good cook, I'll bet."

"I'd need someone to teach me how."

"That's easy enough. You will see how to make an entire turkey dinner on Christmas Day." Merry enjoyed spending time with him in the kitchen. It was where they seemed to get along the best, a neutral zone in which Merry was the teacher and Jack the student.

"How are you feeling?" Absently she brushed her hand across his forehead, feeling for a fever.

He smiled but didn't stop her.

"Human. I finally feel like I might make it. I wondered for a while."

"Good enough to go to the lutefisk dinner?"

"Only if Vince does."

"That reminds me. I still have to find a Joseph for the Nativity."

"Does everything have to be done by you? The entire community seems to depends on you."

"I have no responsibilities whatsoever the rest of the year. Someone else is in charge of the Fourth of July." She finished her sandwich and took her plate to the sink.

"Right now I can't quit thinking about Greta and her family," Jack admitted.

"She got to you too? Greta has that effect on people. She's so sweet and vulnerable."

"And happy, considering what's happening to her family right now."

"One of my coworkers insisted that because Greta wore such ragged clothes to school that she must be abused in some way."

"The child doesn't even know her family is poor!"

"I've realized that my own life wasn't so different from hers." She moved potato chips around on her plate. "I had everything I needed so I assumed that all was well in my world. In fact, the first time I realized that my family might be a little low on the cash totem pole was when my class-mates started getting cars for graduation and I got a check for two hundred dollars for my college fund. Even that was okay, though. I got an academic scholarship that paid for everything but my books."

"Greta is going to be fine."

"I hope so."

"I find it ironic that we always had more money than anyone knew what to do with. That's obvious with this land mess. I never thought about money because it was never an issue." His expression darkened. "And I always had something else to dwell on, absorbed in my own grief."

"So you had all the money you wanted and yet you are unhappy. And Greta's family has nothing and she loves life."

"We're an odd crew—human beings."

"Are you getting all philosophical on me?" Merry teased.

"You're right. I'm better off taking a nap." Jack touched her shoulder gently as he left the room.

His touch caused a delightful but disturbing flutter in Merry's midsection.

Chapter Nineteen

While he slept, Merry waited on last-minute shoppers and thought about Jack.

"You're quiet today," Abby commented. "Not enough business for you?" She referred to the dwindling number of shoppers they had.

"No. This is usually the way it is. People are home wrapping presents and cooking. Business will pick up again on Christmas Eve when people realize they need just one more stocking stuffer or that Aunt Georgette is coming to dinner after all."

"Then what are you thinking about?"

"Jack." She might as well be honest, Merry decided. He was occupying more and more of her thoughts recently. Besides, Abby knew her well enough to deduce the truth anyway.

"You're falling for him, aren't you?" Abby began to straighten a row of elves.

"Is it so obvious?"

"Probably not to anyone but me. Too bad Jack doesn't know his own feelings, let alone yours."

"What do you mean by that?" Abby's discernment surprised her.

"He's attracted to you, but I'm not sure he's comfortable with it. Don't you notice that he'll take your hand or put his arm around your shoulders and then, when he realizes what he's done, he pulls away like you're a hot coal? He's trying to control himself around you."

"No, I can't say I have." Merry felt a little thrill of pleasure at the idea.

"That's why you are so perfect for each other!" Abby crowed. "You're both clueless about your emotions. All you think about is Christmas, and all he is interested in is his work. Once you both wake up and realize what's going on, I'll bet you won't be able to stay away from each other!"

"When I wake up from a nightmare?"

"No, to a dream come true. You'll see."

"You are a hopeless romantic, Abby. Plus, you have a marvelous fantasy life. How about using some of that mental energy on something important—like who will I find to play the part of Joseph in the Nativity? I've got college kids for the five to six and seven to eight o'clock slots, but no one in between when the most people are arriving at the church for dinner. I've asked everyone except the men in walkers and wheelchairs and those who need portable oxygen to get around. I'm getting desperate!"

They heard a creak on the stairs as Jack made his way down. He'd fallen asleep again. That much was evident from the pillow crease across his cheek. He looked up to see them staring at him. "What are you looking at?"

Merry and Abby exchanged a triumphant look. "You!"

"You must have better things to do."

"Not right now," Merry corrected him. "Jack, do you have long johns with you?"

He smiled a little. "That's a pretty personal question, isn't it?"

"Warm clothing, then."

"Yes."

"Did you feel any ill effects after being on the porch to watch the parade?"

"None that I've noticed."

"Then is it possible . . . just possible . . . that you'd be able to stand outside the church for a little while tomorrow night?"

"And expose myself to the elements? What kind of nurse are you?" His expression was teasing.

"I'm desperate, okay? And other than being weak, you're back to your normal self. Will you be Joseph for the living Nativity? It's important that it look realistic while people are coming to the dinner. When the crowd subsides, I have younger guys to fill in."

"Why don't you use them for everything?"

Merry flushed. "Because I'm playing Mary, mother of Christ, and I need someone my own age to balance things out. A pimply high school kid will not look like my Joseph."

"So vanity has crept into the holiday."

Merry turned a deeper red and swatted at him. He ducked.

"You'll do it for me, won't you? We'll put a heater in the manger so you don't get cold. Away from the hay, of course."

"I'll bet the real Mary would have liked that."

"Now you're teasing. Please?"

"What a great idea!" Abby chortled. "He'll fit the shepherd's robes perfectly. Just don't let the goat chew on the hem like last year."

"Do you think I'm nuts?" he asked in disbelief. "Me? The one who thinks Christmas should be a solemn, reverent affair?"

"What's more solemn or reverent than this? I saw a living Nativity when I was a child, and I never forgot it. It's the first time I realized that Jesus was a living, breathing person just like me. He wasn't an angelic figure floating among the clouds, but a kid like me! He had a mother and father, was born and died. He's real! If you can do that for some child, you'll represent Christmas in the most wonderful way possible."

He was weakening, she could tell.

"Oh, for heaven's sake . . ." he growled.

"Yes," Merry agreed solemnly, "it is."

* * * * *

Merry trudged across the yard between her house and Hildy's. The path they usually kept open—from back door to back door—had filled in a little, which meant neither had been traveling it enough. She was worried about her neighbor. Hildy came every day to help in the shop but said little. She walked as if the heaviness of the world's greatest issues had fallen onto her shoulders. Hildy might not be young in years, but Merry saw her turning old in spirit before her very eyes.

Hildy was slow to answer the door. When she did, her gray hair was mussed and her face slack from sleep.

"I didn't mean to wake you."

"It's good you did. I've been sleeping most of the day. I just can't seem to keep my eyes open."

Merry knew that was a sign of the depression Hildy seemed to be sinking into.

"What's wrong, Hildy? We're friends. You can tell me."

"It's something I don't talk about, and I don't care to start now. I hope you understand. This is mine to deal with, honey, but thanks for caring."

"Anytime you change your mind, let me know. I'm here for you."

Hildy patted Merry's hand and invited her inside for tea but never raised the subject again.

She told Jack and Vince about the conversation over dinner.

"People deal with things differently," Jack responded curtly. "It's not our business to try to change that."

"But what if it's destructive? Then they hurt even more than they already suffer."

"Christ knows not only our thoughts but our answers. The rest of us are just flailing around in the dark and may do more harm than good." By the tone of his voice he was obviously referring to those who'd tried to help him in the past.

"You two are going to have to agree to disagree," Vince said with a sigh. "Your life experiences are just too different."

"If I had Jack's experience I believe I'd want help! I don't understand . . ."

Jack laid his hand over Merry's. "Vince is right. Let's just agree to disagree, okay?"

She sputtered to a halt. She'd never understand this man! She could see how she could love him, but understand him? Never!

I could love Jack!

Chapter Twenty

. . . .

"Are you sure you're warm enough?" Merry fretted as she tied a burlap sash around Jack's waist. They were in the church's family room, preparing for their turn at the living Nativity.

"I'm going to be pouring with sweat if you make me wear one more thing," he grumbled. "And I'm sure Joseph never wore a turtleneck sweater."

"It doesn't show under the costume," she assured him as she handed him the triangularly folded square of woolen cloth he would wear secured with a circlet on his head. "Do you want to put another stocking cap on under that?" She stood there in her humble garments, looking remarkably sweet and innocent.

Jack knew better. Beneath her shawl lay a bright and devious mind that had somehow convinced him that the thing he wanted to do most was play Joseph. He still wasn't quite sure how it had happened. Vince had taken her side, and Jack had finally given in. Jack struggled with the headgear until it seemed acceptable and mentally lambasted his friend.

"You look very handsome." Merry's voice was pleased and breathless. "How do I look?"

Jack looked up, and his heart lurched. She looked like an angel. Across from him, on the wall, was a large mirror. They actually did look like a couple from two thousand plus years ago—poor, bewildered, perplexed about their next move, hoping to find a place to have their baby. Something unfamiliar twisted inside Jack.

He believed. He had for as long as he could remember, but seeing someone—even himself—play out the part of the bemused Joseph, the man who had obediently taken a pregnant teenaged wife, was more powerful than he could have imagined. He'd always had faith, but this . . .

Maybe this wasn't such a dumb idea after all. . . .

"Come on, we're up next." Merry tugged on his hand and pulled him to the door.

It wasn't until then that Jack noticed Vince standing in the doorway, taking photos with his cell phone.

"Knock it off!" Jack barked.

Vince only grinned. "Are you kidding? Nobody back home will believe this if I don't have pictures."

Jack mentally put "confiscate camera" on his to-do list.

* * * * *

The barnlike enclosure for the Nativity scene was warmer than Jack had expected. Bales of hay lined the walls and surrounded a tiny crèche. The floodlights, which lit the scene, gave off some heat. The animals warmed the area with their body heat as well—two contented cows munching on hay and a billy goat that wandered around inspecting items that might be edible. There were also assorted dogs lazing about chewing rawhides the pastor had distributed to prevent chaos. The ferret was ensconced in his cage on a hay bale.

As Merry positioned Jack near the manger, he commented, "I'm surprised how comfortable it is."

"It's the animals," Merry told him as she adjusted the tie at his waist. "I've been told that barns start to deteriorate when they no longer hold animals. The creatures give off enough body heat to keep the floors warm and prevent them from frosting up and heaving in the winter. Once they are abandoned, however, the frozen ground takes over."

"A genuine example of 'if you don't use it, you lose it,'" Jack marveled.

"We don't appreciate God's creatures nearly enough," Merry said thoughtfully. "We don't appreciate *Him* enough either. At least we have Christmas to remind us again and again of the Gift we've been given."

Jack couldn't disagree. He'd found himself softening a little about Merry's approach to Christmas. Even though it was a somber, reflective time for him, he did see some merit in her attitude. That alone was a big leap for him.

When she was done fussing with the setting, Merry came to stand beside him.

"Aren't you forgetting something? Where's the baby Jesus? Didn't I see the doll lying on the couch in the family room?"

"We've got a special delivery," Merry said. "Here he comes now."

A young woman with long dark hair walked toward them with the most beautiful baby Jack had ever seen. She laid the child in Merry's arms. The child had a perfectly round face, pink lips that formed a sweet bow, and dark eyes with long, thick lashes. As Jack stared, the baby put his thumb in his mouth and began to suck, relaxing immediately in Merry's arms.

The baby's mother draped a brown fuzzy blanket over the child so that the only portion of the snowsuit that showed was the bit of white around the baby's head, which looked ever so much like a halo.

"I'll be back to pick up Matthew after my husband and I have had our lutefisk," the young woman said. "Thanks for watching him."

"Thank *you*," Merry responded. "He's a beautiful baby Jesus."

Will surprises ever cease? Jack wondered.

Merry cuddled the baby to her chest and nestled against

Jack's side. He felt the warmth of her as she fit into the curve of his arm. He could feel her swaying slightly, the natural response to holding a baby in one's arms, and heard her humming softly.

Away in a manger . . .

Emotions of all sorts coursed through him as he embraced her and the baby. Protectiveness, gratitude, humility . . . love.

Jack stiffened and Merry glanced up at him, but the baby snuffled and quickly drew her attention away.

He was oblivious to the people walking by them as they entered the church. He heard nothing but Merry crooning to the baby and the child's happily gurgled responses. He saw nothing but a soft curl peeking out from beneath Merry's headdress, the sweet profile of her gentle features, and the eyes of the baby, dark and adoring, staring up at her.

The lurch in his stomach should have knocked him off his feet. He was holding the very things he'd never thought he'd have. A beautiful, loving woman, a precious child, a life. Though he hadn't known it at the time or even put two and two together as an adult, those were the things he'd denied himself after his brother had died. Jamie would never know adulthood, and somehow in his childish mind, Jack had decided he wouldn't either. He'd cut himself off from everything but work, denied himself the happiness that he might have had, and lived a life that had its own deadness.

All this flooded over him as he stood in the cocoon of the Nativity scene. One of the cows mooed, and the goat brushed against his leg. Merry still swayed gently with the baby in her arms, rhythmically bumping against him . . .

This was the spirit of Christmas. This was life. This was all he'd denied himself.

The realization hit Jack so hard his knees nearly buckled, and a sense of grief so deep it rivaled that of the days after Jamie's death washed over him. What had he done? He was no more guilty of Jamie's death than Jamie himself. They'd been children, shortsighted, silly kids with more bravado than brains. They'd been like every other young boy was at some time or another—only the consequences for their actions had been so much greater. Sadly his parents had been too deep in their own pain to get any help for his.

He closed his eyes and bowed his head. *Lord, You've forgiven me. How can I forgive myself?*

There, in the makeshift manger, with Merry crooning to the infant, Jack received a gift so big, so miraculous, that he could barely take it in. *"You are forgiven. You've always been. You just have to receive it."*

He hoped no one noticed that Joseph had tears running down his cheeks.

Jack had collected himself by the time Vince came by.

"I'll wait for you guys inside," he said quietly so he didn't distract those around him. "I refuse to eat my first-ever lute-fisk alone."

"Five minutes," Merry murmured. "Then our replacements will come."

They'd been standing there for almost an hour? Jack marveled. Is that all the time it had taken to turn his life upside down and inside out? To finally make him understand how he'd allowed guilt and grief to take his own life much as that tree and sled had taken Jamie's?

As they stepped out of the Nativity scene, Jack felt as if he were stepping into a brand-new world, one with brighter lights and sounds, the life he could . . . no, *should* . . . have been living.

Beside him, Merry returned the angelic baby to its mother.

"He was absolutely perfect," Merry was saying. "Barely a peep out of him."

As the women chatted, Jack stared at the baby. He'd never really paid much attention to babies before tonight. That was part of the life he'd denied himself . . . but no longer.

The child, obviously sensing Jack's interest, bestowed on him a radiant toothless smile that made his entire tiny body wiggle.

Smiling all the way down to one's toes. Until that moment, Jack hadn't realized that was possible. He felt his own smile building within him. Forgiven—by God and finally by himself. There was much to smile about.

Merry, completely oblivious to what had been going on in Jack, tugged on his hand. "Let's get some of these clothes off and join Vince."

He had no time to draw her aside. Vince entered the room.

"You two made quite a couple," he said. There was an odd tone in his voice. Jack glanced at him sharply. "I saw a side of my friend Jack that I hadn't seen before."

"What was that?" Merry asked as she ran a brush through her hair.

Jack stilled, wondering what Vince would say.

"I'm not sure. I've never really thought of him as a father, but he was a pretty good one tonight. And there was something else that I can't quite put my finger on." Vince frowned, deep in thought. He caught Jack's eye. "It was as if something came over you. You looked relaxed, at ease . . . at home, somehow."

Something *had* come over him. Peace. For the first time since he was twelve years old, he felt peace.

Chapter Twenty-One

The room smelled like a fish market. The aroma of fish mingled with the earthy smell of boiling potatoes and the sweet odors of hot apple cider, fragrant baked goods, and hot coffee. It was an overload for the senses.

Women in the kitchen hovered over huge pots of boiling water, staring into them intently, watching for some unspoken signal that told them the lutefisk was ready. Then it was scooped out of the water with strainers and plopped onto large plates, which the men designated as waiters promptly carried to the dining room, where they were accosted by eager diners who were ready for seconds.

Meanwhile, everyone in the line in which Jack and Vince stood took turns at the kitchen pass-through getting their first helpings.

Jack turned to Vince to say something and immediately noticed the strange, greenish cast to his friend's complexion. "Are you okay?"

"What's that?" Vince pointed to a plate of opaque, gelled flesh as it went by.

"That's what we've come for, lutefisk," Merry said.

"No way. I've cleaned stuff like that off the bottom of an aquarium."

"It's hardly that bad." They reached the front of the line, where Merry took a blob of fish, two potatoes, and green peas. Then she poured a quarter cup melted butter over the top. She handed it to Vince. "Try this."

"I could eat my spare tire if it had that much butter on it . . . or is that the point?" Jack asked.

Merry smiled at him prettily and didn't answer. Instead she took rolled lefse from a platter and put it on Vince's plate. Then she got her own plate, and Jack followed suit. Vince didn't move. He just stared down at the food in dismay.

When they sat down, hot coffee magically appeared in paper cups. Then a fresh tray of sweets was settled in front of the trio.

Merry patted Vince's arm. "Dig in."

Jack, aware of his opportunity to show Vince how things were done, and that he, at least, wasn't afraid of a pile of fish gelatin, slopped the butter around on his plate and took a bite of the fish. It slid around in his mouth a bit, as if it couldn't get traction on his tongue. When he did get a bite between his teeth, it had a faintly rubbery texture, which seemed appropriate considering the slimy coating. He swallowed quickly.

"Salt it, and when you take a bite of fish, take some potato too." Merry demonstrated. "Yum."

He wouldn't go that far, Jack thought. It was definitely an acquired taste, but he did have a second helping with more butter, potatoes, and a spoonful of peas. He was drinking coffee and eating butter cookies when Vince, who'd finally forced down a bite, excused himself from the table.

"I'll make him a ham sandwich when we get home," Merry said. "At least he tried it. And you"—she beamed—"are being a good sport!"

"My father did a lot of fishing. We ate it several nights a week. It wasn't such a stretch for me as for Vince. He's suspicious of any seafood but breaded fish sticks."

Jack glanced up to see a man with an angry expression striding toward their table.

"Hi Harry," Merry said. "Merry Christmas. I'd like you to meet—"

Harry interrupted her rudely. He was glaring at Jack. "Just what is it you think you're up to?"

Jack was startled. "Wha—"

"I heard how you guys have been messing around the courthouse, looking at deeds and titles, you and that sleazeball attorney you've got with you. Something funny is going on, and I know you've been looking at the paperwork on my property. Keep your nose out of my business. Just because some relative of yours founded this town doesn't mean you have the right to dig around in our affairs."

Then he looked sourly at Merry. "I don't know why you're encouraging these guys, Merry, but I'm disappointed in you." Harry spun on his heel and stomped off, leaving those at the table gaping after him.

Jack pushed away from the table to go after him, but Merry put her hand on his sleeve. "Don't."

"Did you hear what he said to you? He's disappointed in you? That's ridiculous! You have nothing to do with it. He needs to be straightened out."

"I also heard what he said about you." Merry spoke softly, forcing Jack to sit down beside her in order to hear her words. "What's that about?"

"I think this is something that I, the designated slea-zeball, started," Vince said as he returned to the table. The color was back in his face now that he had something other than his food to think about. He'd heard the conversation.

"A recording mistake was made at the courthouse years ago. Correcting the error will have ramifications. It's going to upset the apple cart around here for a while. Of course, the people involved never did own the Frost land, but it's going to be a real blow when they find out."

"Can't you do something?"

"It's not their property," Vince interjected. "In actuality

it never was. It's Jack's property and his inheritance. What's more, he intends to make sure his cousins' families get their fair share. He's not thinking of himself."

Jack remained silent, his face stoic.

Her shoulders sagged.

Jack cleared his throat. "I think it's time for us to leave, what do you say?"

Merry shook her head. "You guys run along. I have to stay here and help clean up, collect the Nativity costumes, and return the goat. I'll be along as soon as I can."

Jack heard her unspoken message loud and clear. *Not now, not with you.*

Vince stood up and gestured for Jack to do the same.

Reluctantly Jack pushed away from the table. "Do you need help?"

"No. Just go. I'll be there soon." Merry rose and hurried toward the kitchen before Jack could say more.

He and Vince walked silently toward the Christmas boutique, snow crunching beneath their feet.

It was Vince who spoke first. "I'm taking care of this, Jack. You'll have to trust me. The errors were found and the corrections have been made. It's as simple as that. There's nothing illegal or underhanded about what we're doing. In fact, it's long overdue."

"But if it hurts Merry's friends or her standing in the

community . . ."

"Merry will be fine. Everybody loves her. We can all see that. Besides, this has nothing to do with her. It's Frost family business, no one else's."

"I love her, you know."

The words were out of Jack's mouth before he could stop them.

"It's pretty obvious." Vince continued to trudge through the new snow, which had just started falling.

"You *know*? How . . ."

"The way you look at her, the way you two relate to each other. I've never seen you this open or transparent, even vulnerable, before. She's brought you out of that shell in which you'd encased yourself. This is the first time I think I've ever seen you truly happy. When you are with Merry you are the guy you would have been if not for the accident."

Stunned, Jack stopped in the middle of the street. "You can see all that?"

"I'd have to be blind not to." Vince slapped him on the shoulder. "Congratulations, man. Welcome back to the world we live in."

"Do you think Merry . . . Does she . . . Can she . . . ?"

"Love you? It certainly seems so, but she's so nice to everyone that it's hard for any of us not to feel that Merry loves us. Of course, there is that way she looks at you . . . and touches you . . . and . . ."

"She looks at me? How?"

"She's always trying to figure you out. I can see it in her eyes. When I first arrived and you were sick, she was practically ill with worry. I've never seen another woman fuss over a guy like she fusses over you."

"But how does she look at me?"

"Like you're a knight in shining armor mostly. Until tonight. She was pretty upset that we might be causing the people of Frost some inconvenience or worse. I hope she doesn't think you're the villain in all this. I wouldn't worry about it though. She's pretty crazy about you."

"But I am worried. I wouldn't do anything to hurt Merry." Jack felt an unusual frisson of alarm running through him. He'd rarely cared about much of anything in the past, but the thought of losing Merry before he even really had her in his life was terrifying.

"Jack, you aren't hurting Merry. This is purely business and you know that better than anyone. Just stand back and let me do what I do best. We'll have things straightened out before the New Year."

Jack felt a stone growing in his gut. That was less than two weeks away. Was that how long he had to convince Merry that he meant her town no harm—and that he loved her?

* * * * *

When Merry wasn't home by ten o'clock, Jack began to worry. Vince, unconcerned, had turned in, leaving Jack to stew and pace. Even Peppy and Eggnog had fallen asleep on the couch. Nog had tried to cozy up in Jack's lap but had finally given up when Jack persisted on jumping up to look out the window. Maybe he should go to the church to see if she was okay. Or he could just call her, if he could only find the telephone book. Merry carried every phone number in town in her head.

At eleven, he heard her laughing at the front door and raced to open it.

On the top step stood Merry and Zeke. She was smiling broadly at something Zeke had said, and he was reaching for her hand in an intimate gesture.

They all froze in an awkward tableau.

Merry was the first to move. "Jack, are you still up?"

"I was waiting for you." *To tell you I love you.*

"Zeke came in just as we were wrapping up. Fortunately we had food enough for him, but he got stuck putting away tables and folding chairs. I'm so glad he was around. He even returned the goat!"

If he'd ever had a more surreal conversation, he couldn't remember it. Here they were, another man with the woman Jack loved, discussing the return of a farm animal to its rightful owner. All Jack wanted to do was kick Zeke off Merry's front step.

Merry, oblivious to the dirty looks that Zeke was sending Jack, gave her old friend a hug. "Thanks a bunch, Zeke. I owe you coffee for this one."

"Just coffee?" Zeke teased.

Jack wasn't sure if it was for Merry's sake or his own that Zeke had said it.

He also realized that Zeke wanted him to give them some privacy, but Jack wasn't feeling very generous. He held his ground as Merry entered the house.

She turned back to wave at Zeke. "G'night!"

Merry peeled off her gloves and unwrapped the scarf around her neck. "You didn't have to stay up. I don't want you to have a relapse from the cold weather and a late night."

"I'm not a kid anymore, Merry." Now on so many levels he knew that was true.

"Sorry. I just like to nurture people, I guess." She flopped onto the couch and patted the seat. "Tell me what Vince thought of the lutefisk."

Jack dropped down beside her. His greater weight caused her to lean slightly in his direction, and their shoulders brushed. "Not much. I've never seen him green around the gills before."

"But you ate it. The ladies in the kitchen were pleased."

"In the kitchen? People were watching me from the kitchen?"

"Of course. That's life in a small town."

Her smile faded. "You probably noticed that Harry seemed well informed about your business in town."

"About that . . ."

"You aren't going to do anything that will cause trouble, are you?"

"I've turned everything over to Vince to handle. He's one of the best legal minds I've ever met. I'm just fortunate that he holds two capacities in my firm—officer and attorney. He has integrity and compassion. He'll take care of things as well as anyone can."

"But the people on your land . . ."

He put a finger to her lips and found them to be warm, dry, and very kissable. "Shhh . . ."

She went limp. "Trust God and Vince, right?"

"You've got them in the right order."

After Merry excused herself and went to bed, Jack remained in the living room surrounded by the ornaments and Christmas displays he'd so despised. Only the lights from the tree remained on, and the entire room winked and sparkled with light playing off bits of silver and gold. Occasionally the Santa on the floor by the fireplace would detect movement and belt out "Ho, ho, ho!" The cat, who always waited for Jack to go to bed, now didn't even open an eye at the sound. They were all inured to the season.

His thoughts drifted back to early evening and the simple but powerful Nativity scene of which he'd been a part.

People had laughed and talked as they walked toward the church, but everyone had slowed and paused before the tableau and grown silent. Mary, Joseph, the babe . . . so powerful were those images that they silenced the crowds with the reminder of what Christ had come to earth to do.

A stirring of regret moved within him. He'd shut out Christmas so long. Now, because of Merry, the good memories of the season were finally returning—their family going to candlelight services on Christmas Eve, saying grace over a gigantic golden turkey blossoming with dressing and a table laden with mashed potatoes, gravy, candied yams, and the green bean casserole he and Jamie had loved so much. And the gifts they'd exchanged—reminders, his mother had told them, of the gift of His life that Christ had given them.

Wagons, art sets, balls of every size and color, catchers' mitts, pajamas, games . . . it had been good. For the last twenty years he'd forgotten that, replaced it with the few awful minutes that changed his life forever.

But some of the good was returning. Tonight, standing in the cold, depicting the husband of Mary, he'd felt the reality and known deeper in his bones than ever that the story of Christmas was true.

Nog yawned so widely that Jack could see every pearly pinprick of his teeth. The cat rose and stretched, jumped onto the couch, and curled up on Jack's lap.

Feeling the small warm body against him took him back to Merry and the baby, standing close to him so as to share their body heat. He recalled the infant sleeping in her arms, his small mouth working, dreaming, no doubt of warm milk and his mother's smiles. He'd never felt so protective toward another human being as he had in that moment. This was what he wanted for himself—Merry, a child of their own, the closeness a husband and wife shared. He wanted another chance at life.

He threw his head back against the couch and groaned. He'd come here for a quick business trip to clean up a few loose ends and he'd lost his heart—and probably his mind—in the process.

Chapter Twenty-Two

"Zeke, you've got to stop talking like this!" Merry hadn't planned to start her morning with an argument, but obviously Zeke had.

"I'm just telling you, Merry, that guy is going to cause a lot of trouble and heartbreak in this town and you'd better get ready for it. Tell him to stay in a hotel here in Blue Earth. Tell him . . . anything!"

"Is that the astute businessman talking or some jealous person who doesn't like my friendship with Jack Frost?"

She could tell by the hesitation before his response that the second answer was the correct one. Had she been wrong about Zeke? Were his feelings still more than platonic? Or had the advent of Jack brought out the worst in him?

"You don't even know him. I do. He's not like that."

His laugh was dry, without humor. "You might think you know him but you don't. He's had his henchman in the courthouse comparing deeds and titles, property tax payments, and who knows what else. What do you think is going to come of that, Merry? Something good? I doubt it. I know you want to think the best of people, but sometimes . . ."

"I don't believe it," she retorted bravely. "Jack wouldn't. You're just miffed because he's still staying at my house. Well, I don't care! He's a paying customer, and so is Vince."

"I never should have called you that night he was looking for a place to stay. . . ."

"Too late. You did. And I appreciate it. Now please don't say any more to me about Jack."

"Don't say I didn't try to warn you, Merry," Zeke said glumly. "I care about you too much to see the pain this guy is going to put your town through."

After she'd hung up the phone, she sat down and stared disconsolately at the street in front of her house. What if Zeke was right after all? She couldn't see how, but he'd planted a niggling, unwelcome seed of doubt in her.

She entertained this bit of misery until she saw Abby come up the sidewalk to work. Merry gave herself a little talk. What was she doing allowing Zeke's unfounded doubts to ruin her day? It was nonsense! Today was Christmas Eve, and she didn't have the time or inclination to think about anything other than that.

"Hey, Merry, how's it going?" Abby pulled off her coat and scarf and smoothed her hair.

"We'll be busy today. All the last-minute shoppers will be out."

"What time are we closing?" That was a subject Abby and Merry debated every year.

"Three o'clock. I'm having people here for dinner at six o'clock, and we'll attend the candlelight service at midnight. Everyone needs to be home with their families by three. I'd get so excited about Christmas that my father would take a vacation day on Christmas Eve so my mother could cook our meal and wrap gifts without my . . . *help.*" Merry made air quotes. "Dad always baked my birthday cake."

"Is Jack around? Maybe he could help wrap presents. Hildy said she had to do some Christmas shopping of her own today."

It was funny, really, to think how far they'd all come. It wasn't so long ago that Abby had tiptoed whenever Jack was around. Now she was asking for him.

"Abby, what kind of man do you think Jack is?"

"Me? Why does it matter what I think?"

"I'm curious, that's all."

"I didn't like him very much at first. He was pretty grim. But now I think he's a really nice guy. I'm not sure what changed him but I like it." Abby's eyes twinkled. "And he's more handsome every day. The more he relaxes, the more he smiles."

Merry couldn't argue with that. "Zeke thinks he's going to cause trouble in Frost."

A shadow flickered across Abby's features. "My husband says that too. He's been hearing rumors, he says, but won't tell me what they are because he doesn't know for a fact they're true."

"I would have said the same not long ago, but I've had the opportunity to spend more time with Jack than anyone else. Even when he was ill, he was a perfect gentleman. And he's shared things with me that have helped me understand him." Jamie, his family, the guilt that plagued him, and the honor he was showing to his cousins by including them in his inheritance.

Merry knew who Jack was. She could trust him. The rumors were just that, rumors. Besides, what could Jack really do that would set Frost on its head?

* * * * *

By the time Jack and Vince returned from the courthouse, the house was filled with the fragrant aroma of baking turkey. All the dishes except the gravy were ready to put in the oven, and the table was set. The men stopped in their tracks to admire the festive table.

Merry, dressed in a simple navy sheath, sat at the table folding napkins. Her blonde hair spilled across her shoulders, and her eyes deepened to emerald when paired with the dress. She wore a fine silver web of a necklace. It was dainty, asymmetrical, and looked like a bit of frost gracing her neck.

Jack had never seen her in much makeup. Her skin was flawless and porcelain by nature and she really needed none, but tonight she'd added blush and a slash of holiday red lipstick. It was quite dramatic against her pale skin.

"Merry?" Vince finally blurted. "You look like a model!"

"How nice of you to say that." She finished the last napkin and stood up. "It's not true, of course, but I accept the lovely compliment anyway."

Jack simply stared at her.

The doorbell rang and Hildy entered on a gust of snow. She was balancing pie holders in her hands and had a cloth bag full of gifts hanging from her arm. "Ho, ho, ho," she said jovially, her disposition much improved for the festivities.

Jack reached for the plastic containers and headed for the kitchen, leaving Vince to help Hildy with her packages and coat.

Merry joined him there with a jar of cranberry relish Hildy had brought in her bag. "I'm so glad to see Hildy smiling tonight."

"Are *you* okay with celebrating Christmas here?" Merry put a hand on her hip and studied Jack's face. "I want you to enjoy it but I don't want to bring up sad memories."

"It's okay. I've come to the conclusion while I've been here with so much time to think that I've mourned Jamie far too long. The accident wasn't any more my fault than his. I could just as well have been on that sled. It's time I let go." He studied her intently. "I apologize in advance if I fail in that quest. I'm stepping out on baby legs here."

She came to him and put her arms around his waist and laid her head against his chest. "It's okay. You're trying." When she looked up at him there were tears in her eyes. "I'm so happy for you. God doesn't leave us. Just remember that. He'll hold you up and He'll hold you together."

"I'm grateful for that and"—Jack hesitated briefly—"and for you."

She sensed he was about to kiss her, but the sound of a car horn interrupted them.

Vince stuck his head into the kitchen. "I think your little family has arrived, Merry." He observed how closely the two stood together and noticed Merry's arms falling from around Jack's waist. His eyebrow went up, and he glanced at the ceiling. "What? Are you pretending there's mistletoe up there?"

Caught, the pair guiltily split apart and followed Vince into the living room.

Wayne entered the house first, a large package in his arms.

"You weren't supposed to bring gifts!" Merry chided.

"The big one is for Greta. We found her a new bike at the secondhand store. It's in good shape and we bought a new basket for it. The rest of the stuff came from the secondhand store too." He blushed. "Maybe by next year we'll graduate to a discount store for gifts."

"I'm here! I'm here!" Greta bounded in. She was barely visible beneath her stocking cap, but her eyes shone. She was carrying a metal tin. "Mom made Christmas cookies. Pecan tassies—her specialty!"

Merry, from the corner of her eye, saw Hildy watching the scene. She'd flinched, Merry noted, at the mention of tassies. How odd.

But Hildy's behavior grew even stranger when Stephanie entered and threw back the hood of her jacket. Hildy's strangled scream filled the room.

Jack was at the older woman's side when she began to crumple, knees buckling, hand clutching her heart. He caught her before she reached the floor and helped her into a nearby chair.

"Should I call 911?" Vince asked. "You do have 911 out here, don't you?"

"Yes!" Merry said.

"No!" Hildy blurted.

Every person in the room appeared baffled except Stephanie, who gasped and ran straight for Hildy and fell into her arms.

"Mommy?" Greta said in a small voice as she watched her mother cry.

"Steph, what's going on?" Wayne hurried to his wife,

but she refused to be pulled away from Hildy.

"Do you still want 911?" Vince asked, looking more confused than ever.

"Do you know what's happening?" Jack asked Merry.

"I'm not sure, but if it's what I think it is, then we're witnessing a Christmas miracle."

Stephanie broke away from Hildy then. Tears streamed down her cheeks, but her eyes shone with happiness. "Wayne, this is Bernice Olson, my former mother-in-law and Greta's grandmother!"

"Grandma?" Greta echoed, understanding dawning on her small features. "My daddy's mother?" She too shot toward Hildy. "Do you remember me, Grandma?"

"Remember you? You are impossible to forget." Hildy started to cry again, and Greta wiped the tears away with a wrinkled tissue from her pocket. "I've missed you so much."

Wayne, stunned, stood there with his hands helplessly flapping at his sides, not knowing what to do next.

It was Vince who finally spoke above the din. "Will someone please tell me what's going on? Do we need an ambulance or a paddy wagon?"

At that, explanations began to tumble out. Hildy told Vince about her son being killed and how'd she'd returned to Frost and taken back her childhood nickname. Stephanie, in tears, explained the horrible two years after her husband's death when she cut herself off from everyone she'd ever known. Then Greta, who hadn't left Hildy's lap, announced, "I'm the happiest kid in the whole world. I got my grandma back!"

Even Vince, whom Merry knew better for his quick tongue than shows of emotion, had tears in his eyes by the time they were done.

As the excitement began to wind down, Merry clapped her hands to her cheeks and gasped, "I almost forgot the turkey! Vince, Jack, you come with me. The rest of you sit down."

Jack grinned at Hildy. "Talk amongst yourselves. I'm sure you can think of something to say." They were babbling happily before he got to the kitchen door.

"That's some story," Vince remarked as he piled mashed potatoes into a serving dish. "It's like a Hallmark Christmas Eve movie made for television."

Merry moved the turkey, golden brown with crisp, succulent skin, to a platter and handed it to Jack. "Will you carve at the table?"

"Me? Wouldn't you do a better job?"

"If it makes you uncomfortable . . ." Merry was disappointed. She'd wanted to see Jack at the head of her table carving the turkey for the people she'd gathered for the night. Maybe it was too much to hope for. They'd already witnessed a Hallmark special. To plan a Norman Rockwell table might be pushing it.

"I'll do it if no one criticizes me if I do it wrong." Jack

sent Vince a warning glance.

After Merry had left the kitchen with the bird, Vince turned to him. "Where did the Grinch learn to carve a turkey?"

"I didn't grow up with a pack of wolves," Jack reminded him. "My father taught me. We still acknowledged Thanksgiving and Easter with a turkey even though we never had a festive Christmas."

"You've changed," Vince commented.

"Who has changed?" Merry poked her head through the door. "If you guys bring those casseroles to the table, we're all set."

"Jack has changed. I've never seen him smile so much in the month of December. I'm sure you have something to do with it, Merry."

She studied the pair of handsome men for a moment. "I've been praying for Jack. Maybe that's it."

"Don't stop now." Vince slapped Jack on the back. "He's got a long way to go."

Everyone was laughing as they seated themselves at the table. An air of expectancy grew as they quieted.

"Jack, will you pray?" Merry asked.

He stared at her. "Me?"

"If you don't want to . . ."

"No, it's okay." He drew a deep breath.

"Heavenly Father, there's much to thank You for. First

there is the gift of Your Son. There aren't words enough to thank You for that. Thank You for this mouthwatering food, this place to gather, and for the miracle reunion we saw unfold. I personally thank You for my friendship with Vince, irritating as he can be sometimes, and for Merry, who has been a powerful force in so many lives, including mine."

He lifted his eyes slightly, and Merry caught him looking at her.

"'Thank You for giving me people who finally got me to see that Christmas is all about new birth, life, and joy. May all of us experience it tenfold over the coming year."

When he'd said "amen," Jack looked up again and was surprised to see tears on Merry's cheeks and even more shocking, on *Vince's*.

Fortunately neither had to explain because Greta, in her most polite yet impatient voice, inquired, "Is anyone ever going to pass me the turkey?"

Chapter Twenty-Three

Merry barely touched her food, although the others seemed to inhale it. Instead, she filled herself with the sights and sounds of the festive table. This was what it was to have family, not blood family but family nonetheless, celebrating this wonderful evening together. The day she'd longed for as a child had finally come and filled the void that had left her incomplete for many years. What could be better than this?

Hildy was smiling. Ten years had fallen away and the light had returned to what Merry had come to think of as old, sad eyes. Stephanie and Wayne were giddy with happiness. They had found Hildy, made new friends, and put their feet on the path to a new life. Greta beamed as only a small child can. She wiggled and giggled, talked a blue streak, and her body practically shivered with happiness.

Vince, too, was part of her family now, Merry thought. She'd seen the warm, thoughtful side of his personality and his loyalty to Jack.

Jack . . .

Merry feasted her eyes on him. All the gravity and unease was gone from his demeanor. The tense, brooding man who'd entered her home only a couple brief weeks before was replaced by a man filled with laughter and goodwill. His cheerful mien made him look different as well. He was relaxed in both posture and dress. He'd traded suits for jeans and soft sweatshirts. He'd given up taming his dark hair and allowed the soft curl to reveal itself. It was longer, too—an especially good look for him.

And his smile! Merry had thought he was incredibly handsome when they'd first met, but now he was spectacular.

She blushed when she caught Jack staring back at her and hoped that he hadn't somehow developed mind reading as a new skill.

"Aren't you going to eat more than that, Merry?" Hildy asked in a motherly but disapproving tone. "You'll fade away."

"I'm saving myself for dessert. It's going to be wonderful, wait and see."

As she pushed away from the table, so did Jack.

"Everyone else relax. I'll clear the table so Merry can prepare the next course."

She put a hand on his arm gratefully. They made a good team in the kitchen. By the time the dishes were cleared and coffee poured, Merry was done whipping cream and serving slices of pie—pumpkin, mincemeat, apple crumble, cherry, lemon meringue, and pecan.

"There's enough here for each of us to have our own pie!" Jack eyed the pie plates on the counter.

"Hildy brought four, and I whipped up the other two. I want this to be the most memorable Christmas you've ever had." She paused before adding, "In a good way that is."

"It's already that." His voice was low and husky. He moved toward her, and Merry knew he was going to kiss her and that she was going to welcome it.

Jack hesitated, however, at a tinkling sound coming from the dining room. The guests were tapping spoons against their glasses to signal they wanted dessert.

"We aren't at a wedding party," Merry muttered, "and the bride won't be kissing the groom." She felt a burn of embarrassment scorch its way across her cheeks. "I mean . . ."

"You take that tray and I'll take this," Jack suggested, saving her from more awkwardness.

Mercifully, if anyone noticed Merry's red face they didn't comment.

"Shall we open gifts after dessert?" Merry suggested. "If we don't start soon, we'll be late for the candlelight service at church."

Hildy cleared her throat. "If you don't mind, Merry, we'll take ours home this evening. Rather than go to church this evening, I think we need some family time. Stephanie and Wayne have agreed to stay with me tonight so the four of us can go to church together in the morning." Her voice cracked with emotion. "Although I've already received my gift in Greta and Stephanie." She looked at the young man sitting next to her daughter-in-law. "And Wayne. I think we need a little time to get to know each other."

"Take all the time you need. I'll pack up some turkey and stuffing for you so you don't have to cook tomorrow."

While Hildy and family put on their coats, Merry filled a basket with portions of everything she'd served tonight.

After kisses, hugs, and more tears, they left. Merry, Jack, and Vince stood in the doorway and watched them trudge across the snow to Hildy's house.

"Extraordinary," Vince finally said. "I can't believe it went down like this—supposed strangers meeting on Christmas Eve—and turning out to be long-lost family members! Truth *is* crazier than fiction."

They sat in front of the fire to open their gifts. Vince handed them each an envelope and looked a little sheepish. "I shopped online. Sorry it isn't fancy but you both need it."

Merry put her finger beneath the flap and tore it open, unable to imagine what it was Vince thought she needed. She opened the trifolded piece of paper inside. Her jaw dropped as she read it.

One airline ticket to the North Pole or destination of your choice.

It's time you took a vacation.
Merry Christmas, Vince.

"You shouldn't have! It's too much. I didn't get you anything like . . ."

"Accept it graciously, Merry. I have it to give."

She saw the intensity on his face and nodded. "Vince, this is amazing and I thank you so much. I've never actually had a real vacation, unless you count spring breaks in college and I hated those."

"Much better. Enjoy it. If you want to go to the North Pole and see Santa it's okay with me, but I'm thinking of something more like Florida, Sanibel Island, or Naples, for example. Your choice."

She hugged the paper to her chest. "This is going to be fun!"

Merry picked up a box and handed it to him. "Now it's your turn. It's not much and it's really kind of silly, but at least it will remind you of this Christmas."

"Whatever it is, it's perfect," Vince assured her. The tissue paper fell away and a startled look passed across his features. Carefully he lifted a quilt out of the box. Each square featured a different Christmas scene.

"I just pieced the top," Merry hurried to explain. "I didn't have time to back and quilt it, but I will. Then I'll send it to you. On those days when even California feels damp and chilly, you can use it to take a nap on your couch and think of tonight."

"When did you manage to do this?" Vince asked. His throat was full and his voice unsteady.

"At night, after you guys went to bed. It's a simple nine-patch pattern. I was just afraid you might hear my sewing machine and wake up. I put the machine in my closet and used it in there. That's as far away as I could get from your rooms."

"You did this in a closet?" Jack asked. "Just so Vince would be surprised?"

"It worked, didn't it?" She gave him a bright smile.

Vince seemed truly moved by her gesture. "I never expected anything like this. I'll treasure it."

He offhandedly tossed a similar envelope at Jack. "Here's something for you too."

Inside was a note indicating that Jack now had season tickets for the LA Lakers. He whistled appreciatively. "You expect me to take time off to attend all these games?"

"I do. You've got to ease up, buddy, or you'll run out of steam far too young. I know you've never cared about that, but I do." Vince's gaze flickered toward Merry and back again. "Other people who love you do too."

His smile wavered a little but Jack said, "You know, I might have been wrong about ignoring Christmas. I'm beginning to like this part, the gift-giving, I mean."

"Good, because I have something for you too." Merry went to the back of the tree against the wall and dragged a package toward Jack. His box was considerably bigger and heavier.

"What do we have here?" he asked as he untied the ribbon and ripped away the sparkling red-and-green wrapping paper.

"I have something to confess first." Merry looked worried. "Your gift is something I started a long time ago, before I knew you, Jack, but it seemed like the right present to give you. I'd planned to make something special just for you, but—and I'm not sure why—I felt like this should be yours."

He peeled back layers of tissue to expose another quilt. This one was flannel and much larger and far more detailed. It depicted scenes of lakes and rivers, bears and bison, deer and turkeys, canoes and kayaks. There was intricate appliqué on each square. The colors were so rich and inviting that one could snuggle into the quilt and get lost in it.

"It's scenes of Minnesota," Merry explained unnecessarily. "Minnesota as I see it, at least. And I hand quilted it."

"You made every stitch by hand?" Jack ran his hand across the softness.

"Yes, I did."

"I can't take this. It's too special. You worked on it so long."

She waved her hand in the air, dismissing his statement. "This is Christmas, my favorite time of year. One of the things I love most is blessing people with gifts. You'll make me sad if you don't take it."

Doubt played on Jack's features.

"Please?"

"You mean it will hurt you if I don't take this beautiful thing?"

"Yes. To the core."

He sighed and pulled out the weighty comforter. As it bloomed out of the box it was even more beautiful. "I don't know what to say."

"Say thank you," Merry teased.

"Thank you, a hundred times, thank you."

She sat back looking pleased.

"Merry," Jack said, "I understand that this is something you've been working on for a very long time. May I ask what you'd initially planned for it?"

She didn't answer for a long time, weighing the pros and cons of telling him the truth. Truth, as usual with Merry, won out.

"I made it for my trousseau, my hope chest, that old-fashioned thing women don't do anymore. But I'm an old-fashioned girl at heart, and I decided to make something I thought my future husband would like—fishing, hunting, you know. When I didn't marry, I began to use the other things I'd put in there like my dishtowels, sheet, and pillowcases. I was never quite sure what to do with the quilt until this week. I knew in my heart that I wanted to give it to you for Christmas."

She looked at the expression on Vince's face and laughed. "I didn't give it to him in hopes of snaring him for myself, Vince. I did it because I couldn't *not* give it to him. Jack needs it. He lost so much."

She turned back to Jack. "Call it a healing quilt, if you will."

She hadn't known how Jack would receive her gift, but she'd been compelled to give it. Sometimes God put in her impulses she couldn't ignore. This had been one of them. Thankfully Jack received it graciously.

Jack stared at Merry for a long while before nodding.

He dug in his pocket and pulled out a small wrapped gift. "This doesn't look like much after something handmade, beautiful, and so close to your heart."

"Oh, come on!" Vince broke the solemn mood. "Give the girl her present. I want to see what it is."

With a sigh, Jack handed over the small box. "Store-bought. I didn't even do the wrapping, but the sentiment is there."

"I'm sure it is." Merry felt her fingers shaking as she carefully undid the paper. She always saved Christmas wrap to reuse in the store, and this was particularly beautiful.

She felt velvet beneath her fingertips as the small jeweler's box was revealed. She held it to her ear and shook it, but it gave away none of its secrets.

"Open it," Vince encouraged.

When she did, she saw a platinum necklace with the largest, most beautiful diamond she'd ever seen. She ran her finger over the stone before she took the necklace out of its box and held it to her neck.

Vince whistled. "Good job, Jack. That's a beauty."

Merry cradled the necklace in her hands and said nothing. Silently she handed it back to Jack.

"What are you doing?"

"And you said my gift to you was too big! That diamond has to be almost a carat. You could probably buy my store for the money you spent on that, Jack."

"So? Like Vince, I have it to spend. You know my financial situation."

"Why spend it on me?" Tears shone in her eyes.

"Merry," he said intently as Vince's presence receded into the background, "whether or not you know it, you gave me my life back. If it hadn't been for you I'd still be angry, guilty, and living in the past. I didn't believe there was a way to get over Jamie's death and move on. You opened my eyes. Your crazy joy over the holiday, your passionate faith, your giddy pleasure at helping others . . . it was like nothing I've ever experienced. You gave me a gift that no one else has even been able to—I got myself back and, I believe, my life. If that's not worthy of a diamond bauble, I don't know what is."

Vince cleared his throat and stood up. "And now that I've witnessed another miracle, I'm going to bed. See you in the morning for church." He quickly disappeared up the steps.

Jack chuckled. "I don't think Vince is comfortable with gooey stuff."

"Are you comfortable with it?"

"More every day," and he kissed her.

They sat together watching the fire, Merry curled into Jack's chest, his arm around her protectively, as if he'd never let her go. There was such peace in the room that neither felt the need to speak.

It was some time before Jack shifted so he could look at Merry. "I have something to confess."

"Confess away," she purred. "I forgive you for everything."

"Not that kind of confession. I want to tell you when something clicked inside me like a switch turning the light on."

"Hmm?"

"It was when we were playing Mary and Joseph for the living Nativity. I felt you against me and saw the look in your eyes as you studied that baby. It was the first time I truly realized what I've been missing. I've held everyone at arm's length, friends, coworkers, women who expressed an interest in me, everyone."

She sat up and looked into his eyes.

"I realized that I wanted a wife, that I wanted a child, that by carrying Jamie's death on my shoulders I'd denied myself that kind of life. I want that kind of life now, Merry. And I want it with you."

Chapter Twenty-Four

....

They slept late after attending the midnight candlelight service at church. Merry was the first to awake, and she had the coffee brewing when Vince and Jack came downstairs.

"There are rolls and coffee. Church starts at eleven. I'm going upstairs to get dressed." She looked shyly at Jack, wondering if she'd imagined last night. It was almost too wonderful to have been real.

But the intimate, only-for-her smile Jack gave her told her it hadn't been a dream.

Merry was tempted to look down at her toes and make sure she wasn't walking on air.

* * * * *

The church was full with not only the families of Frost but all their Christmas guests. As Merry sat beside Jack, their shoulders rubbing, a sense of peace filled her. It was as if God had planned this moment in time just for her.

Nothing would make her forget this feeling of contentment with her life and her love for—

She snapped back to attention as Pastor Ed began to read the Christmas story and then shared a short message. When he was done, the congregation joined together for several carols. The singing was joyful and robust. At the end of the service, everyone filed out, and each child received a small brown paper sack to take home.

"What's that?" Vince asked. "Do we get one?"

By the time they got to the back of the church to shake hands with the pastor, most of the children had gone. Merry took a bag out of the still overflowing basket and tipped her head toward Vince. "Do you mind, Pastor? Vince wonders what's inside."

"Help yourself," Pastor Ed said. "By the way, Hildy called to tell me what happened. Praise God!"

He turned to Jack, then Vince. "Christmas blessings to both of you."

By the time they got back to Merry's, Vince was digging into the paper sack. He took it to her kitchen table and removed the contents piece by piece.

"Peanuts in the shell, an orange, peppermints, hairy candy . . ."

"That's ribbon candy. The fuzz is from the peanut shells. It wouldn't be the same if everything didn't melt together a little under the lights."

"But what is it?"

"A treat for the children. Fifty or sixty years ago it was a very big deal to hand out these sacks. Sometimes kids didn't get much more than that for Christmas. It's a tradition we've continued. I think it reminds us of how little we need and how much we want."

"I feel like I've stepped back in time." Vince paused. "I'm going to miss it when I head back to California."

Merry glanced at him. "When is that?"

"Yeah, when *is* that?" Jack echoed. "You've kept me in the dark lately as to what you're doing." He scowled at his friend.

"And look how much healthier you look. You have me to thank for it. No stress, no strain."

"Trusting you is both stress and strain, Vince. I need to get back in the loop."

"I'm doing what has to be done and you know it."

The discussion had taken on a somber, ominous tone, Merry noted. Vince was telling Jack to back off so he could do what needed to be done. What, exactly, did that mean?

Merry forgot about it as they drifted through the day, eating leftovers and playing Scrabble. Eggnog and Peppermint got to open their gifts—treats from Merry and toys from Jack.

"I can see whose gift Nog likes best." Merry pretended to pout.

She watched Jack play with the cat. He'd tied a string to a small branch and feathers to the string. The cat chased the feathers and purred loud as a motor until Jack's arm became tired. Then Nog curled up in his lap and fell asleep. For Peppy, Jack had purchased an enormous bag of rawhide bones. The dog disappeared, dragging one of the bones in his mouth, and they heard crunching sounds emanating from behind the couch for the entire afternoon.

"Well?" Vince said to Jack as dusk fell. "How do you rate Christmas this year?"

Merry, who was carrying dishes into the living room so they could eat by the fire, stopped in her tracks.

Jack propped his feet on the footstool and looked thoughtful. The look of distress that was usually present when he considered Christmas was absent. His handsome features were serene, his expression relaxed.

"It's a fresh start. A new beginning. A rebirth, which is fitting considering the other birth we celebrate." His gaze caught Merry's. "A Christmas full of miracles."

Later, alone in her room, Merry's prayers were ones of joyous gratitude.

* * * * *

Jack woke up feeling better than he had in weeks . . . no, months . . . or perhaps years.

Merry greeted him in the kitchen. "You look rested."

"I feel great. Where's Vince?"

"He left a half hour ago." She frowned. "He said something about pulling the trigger on all the work he's been doing." She handed him a mug of coffee. "What does that mean?"

"We told you we had found mistakes in the recording of some deeds and tax rolls from years ago when my great-grandfather was in Frost. Vince thinks that when they computerized, they input the wrong information. It shouldn't have happened, but who knows back then? I'm sure it wasn't intentional."

"What can he do now?"

"The deeds will be updated, and whatever confusion was caused will have to be rectified. Vince is a great attorney and a wonderful business associate who looks out for me. I'm confident that whatever he has done, it's correct." Jack grinned. "I'm learning to enjoy sitting back and letting him do the work."

"Isn't that what he was hired for in the first place?"

"Sure, but I always had a hard time letting go of the reins. Work was all I had. If I wasn't busy, I spent too much time regretting my life."

"And now?"

He put his hands around her waist and pulled her into his lap. "Now I have you to think about. Who needs work?"

He kissed her then. She tasted of cinnamon and strawberry jam. As Merry sank deeper in his arms, Jack couldn't imagine that he could ever be happier.

"What do you think we should do about this?" he murmured, his lips pressed into her hair, eyes closed.

"About what?" She sounded dreamy, content.

"You and me."

"Oh, *that*." She tipped her head back so she could look at him. The expression in her eyes was sheer tenderness and love. "Maybe we need to think about that."

"I don't. I know what I want to do."

He felt her tighten her arms around him.

"I want to marry you." The words were easy to say, smooth and welcome on his lips.

"Oh, Jack . . ." She leaned her head against his chest and buried herself in his warmth. "I want to marry you too."

He kissed her deeply, ardently, and she responded with an eagerness and enthusiasm that surprised him. "You do? Really?"

"You sound surprised."

"I am, a little. I never expected to feel as happy as I do right now." Tenderly, he brushed a stray hair from her eyes. "Or so lucky."

The flavor of her was still on his lips when his cell phone rang.

They both jumped, startled by the piercing sound. Jack wanted to ignore it but knew he couldn't. Vince had told him to be on hand today in case any questions came up.

"Sorry. I promised Vince."

"It's okay. I'll have you forever. I can share you for a minute."

He kissed her nose and punched TALK on the phone.

"Hi. It's Vince."

Vince sounded a little nervous, Jack thought. Odd.

"I know you're thinking about Merry and how she'll respond once she hears that you own . . ." Vince cleared his throat. "Never mind."

"What do you mean, never mind? What were you going to say?"

"Remember that you told me that your great-aunt once lived in Merry's house?"

"Yeah, so?"

"It's still your house, Jack. You also own two lots on the other side of Hildy's place. There's a little house on one lot and the other is empty. And apparently your relative also owned the majority of Main Street. You own all the land on which Frost sat when it was founded. Still, the majority of the confusion involves the farmland. We'll get it straightened out, don't worry."

Jack held a finger in the air, signaling Merry to wait, and then went up to his room to speak privately with Vince.

"What is Merry going to say?" he hissed.

"I know she isn't going to be happy about this, but she's a reasonable woman."

"Merry's passionate about Frost. Even though she understands on a logical level, she's going to resent anything I do to upset its residents."

"I've filed an action to quiet the deed," Vince told him, and Jack winced. An action to quiet the deed was a lawsuit filed in order to discover the real owner of the land in question. "It had to be done, you know that."

"She's going to think we're suing the people of Frost for their land," Jack said miserably. It was the way it was done. There was no hostility in the lawsuit, simply the desire to clear up ownership and misunderstandings. He'd tried to keep it private until everything was straightened out. He'd hoped to have a clear picture of what his cousins would receive before he began talking specifics with anyone else. Would Merry—or the people affected—believe that?

Not likely.

"This is what you came here to do," Vince persisted. "She wasn't even on your radar when you came to town. She'll get over it."

"Will she?"

Vince had no idea how upset Merry would be—or how much her distress mattered to him. He'd just found her. Jack couldn't risk losing her now.

Chapter Twenty-Five

Merry decided to give herself a day off before preparing for her after-Christmas sale. Besides, she wanted to relish the moment that Jack had asked her to marry him. Warmth curled through her at the thought, and she hugged herself. It was impossible to contain her delight.

Jack had gone to the Twin Cities, and Vince had headed toward Blue Earth. She wanted to enjoy this time alone and to imagine herself as *Mrs. Jack Frost. Merry Noel Frost.* What better name could a Christmas girl have? She was destined to run a Christmas shop, she decided right then and giggled out loud.

She hadn't had her feet up for more than ten minutes when her front door slammed open, shaking the window-panes and the unsold baubles still on the Christmas trees.

Harry Conner stormed into the room still wearing his heavy boots and tramping snow everywhere. His hat was pulled low over his eyes, and he was breathing heavily.

"I told you that you should have gotten rid of that fellow!" He waved an envelope in front of her. "You've been harboring a scoundrel right under our noses, Merry, and I don't like it one bit."

She scrambled to her feet to face Harry. First the church and now in her own home he was pestering her with this nonsense. And he'd walked in without knocking! This was her private home, didn't he remember that? What must it have taken to get him this agitated?

"That's enough, Harry. I don't tell you how to run your farming operation. Please don't tell me how to run my B-and-B. And next time, knock."

Harry was so angry he was shaking. His nostrils flared and his pupils were widely dilated. Merry almost felt afraid.

"Maybe you should go now, Harry. We can talk about this when you've calmed down."

"I'm not going to calm down!" he roared. "Nobody sues Harry Conner and gets away with it!"

"You're being sued? For what?"

She was confused now. She could understand his anger if he thought his property was in jeopardy, but what did that have to do with Jack? He'd never said anything about a lawsuit, nor had Vince.

"Wait until you go to the post office, Merry. Maybe you'll get a letter like this too. A lot of people are up in arms. He's trying to take our property away from us. These rich guys only care about getting richer, no matter what it costs the rest of us!"

Merry slipped into her shoes and jacket and followed him out of the house. She waited until Harry had raced away in his pickup to run to the post office, avoiding Regina Olsdorf, who was ranting to the postmaster about something. When she got home, she threw the mail on the table. There, on top of a stack of cards and catalogues, lay a pristine white envelope. The name of someone from Vince's law office was imprinted on the return address.

She began to tremble. Fortifying herself with hot coffee and prayer, she opened the letter. Whatever it said, she hoped it didn't do anything to change her relationship with Jack.

The words on the page swam together as Merry read.

> ... *clear up claims of ownership. . . the plaintiff*
> *Jack Frost . . . names of known claimants must*
> *be notified by mail . . . if no one answers the*
> *complaint, default judgment will be awarded to*
> *the plaintiff . . . any complaints that result will be*
> *a contested legal action . . . outcome determined in*
> *the court . . . your property has been found to be . . .*

Jack was suing her too! And how ironic, he'd done it the day after he'd proposed to her. Could it get any worse than this? Merry didn't think so.

But what was he suing her for? She didn't own the farmland in question, which Jack himself had mentioned.

She had nothing that interested him. The only thing she had, that she took pride in, that she'd earned by her own hard work, was her home and business.

The thought came like a lightning strike, momentarily paralyzing her.

Jack was suing her for the ownership of her home!

Feelings of devastation and betrayal overwhelmed her. *Not Jack, please, not Jack!*

Merry laid her head on the table and wept.

* * * * *

When Jack and Vince arrived almost simultaneously at the house at dinnertime, they found their luggage packed and sitting on the front step.

Jack called to Hildy, who was brushing snow off her car. "Where's Merry? Do you know what's wrong?"

She looked up and it occurred to him that her eyes had that sad look again.

"Oh, she's in the house."

He turned the knob. It was locked.

"What is she doing?" He was genuinely puzzled. This wasn't like Merry. It must be a joke. She was teasing them.

Vince cleared his throat and put his hand on Jack's arm. "About that . . ."

Hildy trudged over to them and gestured at her own house. "I think you'd better come to my place. You can talk there if you want to. Stephanie's family isn't here right now."

Absolutely baffled by everyone's behavior, he and Vince followed Hildy home, leaving their bags right where they were.

Inside was warm and cozy. Most of the furniture featured floral patterns, but it was sturdy and comfortable. They dropped into two chairs and Hildy brought them steaming cups of tea. "You'll need this too. I'll just go in the other room now."

"That's okay. This is your home. You have the right to be here. Maybe Vince can explain this to both of us."

Silently Vince pulled an envelope out of his inside jacket pocket. "I have an idea what's upset her. The PDF of this letter was sent to me today. Without my permission, they were mailed on Saturday so everyone should have gotten one today." Vince grimaced. "I have some very enthusiastic people working for me, but heads will roll over this. They sent this without having my prior approval. I wanted you to read it first. I'm so sorry."

As Jack skimmed the page, his eyes widened. "Vince, this is pretty scary language. All I wanted to do was trace my land, not sue the people of Frost."

"A quiet title suit is a lawsuit but it doesn't have to be contentious. We already know there were errors back in the days before computers. It's just a matter of establishing your right to that property once the errors are corrected. Paperwork, that's all."

"Vince, these are fighting words to people around here. You've been a lawyer so long you are accustomed to this language. These people will believe they are fighting for not only their property but their lives."

"But it's your property, Jack. It always has been. Nothing can change that."

Jack leaned forward, his gaze boring into Vince. "If I take back my property, they'll lose their livelihood."

"I thought you understood that, buddy."

Jack groaned and flopped back in his chair. "No wonder Merry kicked us out. She's probably furious." A horrified expression flickered across his features. "You didn't send her a letter too, did you?"

"I had to. You hold the title to her house. I know you'd just give it to her, but it has to go through the process."

"I'd been meaning to tell Merry that you'd discovered that the house she thought she'd purchased for back taxes wasn't hers at all, but in the excitement about Christmas I didn't bring it up. I thought you understood, Vince."

"You told me to take care of it and I did, legally and properly. You can rent the land back to those farmers. They don't have to move. You aren't planning to come to Minnesota to farm. Nothing has to change except, of course, they'll have to pay you rent for the land. You won't gouge them. Knowing you, you'll give them a great deal."

"But what about the years past?" Jack felt sick to his stomach.

"Everyone has paid taxes on the land. They shouldn't have and you should have. Maybe we can work something out, a year's taxes for a year's rent. We can be as loose or as hard-nosed as we want with this. No worries. I don't think any money will have to change hands if everyone is agreeable."

"Easy for you to say. You don't have your name on a lawsuit against this sleepy little town."

"Once we educate people as to what we're doing and let them know that things won't change that much, things will calm down."

"But they'll no longer own not just their property but their homes!"

Again, Vince shrugged.

Jack had hired him to do what needed to be done and Vince had complied. Jack mentally berated himself for not following this more closely, but he'd been sick . . . and then sick with love for Merry. It was his own fault, and he'd have to bear the consequences.

Hildy cleared her throat. Jack had forgotten she was there.

"Just so you know, I feel much better now."

They both stared at her. "What do you mean?" Vince asked.

"Merry was over here today crying her eyes out. I read the letter and came to the same conclusion she did—that you'd somehow betrayed her and Frost and were turning on all of us. Then I went uptown and walked into a frenzy. They were all at the community center, furious. They were deciding on who to hire as lawyer for their side, planning to tar and feather Jack and saying a lot of things they should be ashamed of in hindsight.

"But listening to you now, it doesn't sound so bad. It is your property, whether the people here like it or not. That won't change, but if you treat them fairly, they should see reason."

"And Merry?"

The sadness in Hildy's eyes deepened, and Jack knew immediately where the unhappiness had come from.

"I don't know about that," Hildy said bluntly. "Your relationship with her might be irrevocably broken. She was devastated."

Heartsick, Jack turned to Vince. "Send out another letter immediately. Explain what we've said here today. Make them understand that I mean to disrupt the community as little as possible." He paused and fell into deep thought. "You know I'd decided to give my cousins their share of the property in farm land. Doing that would allow me to take my share as homesteads and land in the town. Every farmer affected will be given the title to their homestead out of my one-third share. They can keep their houses. We'll settle with back taxes for back rent and call it even."

Jack paced like a caged creature, back and forth across the floor. His mind whirled. "I should have made this all clear in the beginning, but I didn't know these people and I didn't . . ."

"Trust any of them?" Vince filled in the blanks. "You called it the way I would have. And what are you going to do about your property inside the city limits?" Vince asked. "You own a lot of that too."

"Give the houses to the people who live in them. Deed the public property to the city itself so the people can decide what to do with it." He turned to Hildy. "And I'll give that empty house next to yours to Stephanie and Wayne so you can't lose them again."

Tears sprang to her eyes. "I knew what the people were saying wasn't true of you!"

"But will it be enough?" he asked softly.

"That's up to Merry. She's deeply hurt about everything, especially about her house and the fact that you didn't even warn her that this was coming. She thinks you betrayed her."

Jack glared at Vince. "That's because I didn't realize it myself. I turned everything over to Mr. Efficient Attorney's office here."

Vince hung his head. It was obvious that for the first time ever, he was mad at his staff for taking the initiative at work.

Why hadn't he thought about the action to quiet title? Jack wondered. Because it was simply a standard legal measure that needed to be done. He'd meant no harm by it.

"And he did his job, fair and square. Tell her that," Hildy said.

"I will," Jack murmured, "if she will talk to me."

He'd hit the nail on the head, Jack thought as he tried to get Merry to come to the door. He called her but she wouldn't pick up the phone. It went right to voice mail. He rapped on all the downstairs windows, but she'd pulled the shades and drapes tight, too tight for him to see even movement inside the house. Jack had thrown pinecones at the upstairs windows, particularly those of Merry's room, but she didn't look out. For all intents and purposes, the house was empty.

Other than breaking down the door and getting arrested for some infraction or other—and he didn't doubt she'd press charges right now—he was helpless. She had enough food inside those walls to feed herself till spring. She probably set her alarm so she could go to bed and then walk the dog early, under cover of darkness. She could knit, quilt, and bake to her heart's content.

But what about her teaching job?

Jack dialed the number of the school. "This is Jack Frost and I'm wondering what day your kindergarten teachers come back from Christmas break."

He was given a date. Then the secretary added, "Of course, we just had one teacher call in to say she might be taking more time off after the holiday so we will need to find a sub."

"Merry?" he asked.

"Yes." She sounded surprised. "How did you know?"

Jack thanked her and hung up the phone.

So that was the way it would be. At first he was angry but it didn't last long. He began to think about this from Merry's point of view.

He should have told her what he'd intended for the land, but he was so wrapped up in falling in love with her that he'd pushed all that to the back of his mind.

From her perspective he'd asked her to marry him and then stabbed her in the heart.

He looked at the darkened house and felt tears at the backs of his eyes. She wasn't going to come out. Not for him. Not now.

Jack took a deep breath. If he couldn't do anything about Merry, he could at least do his best to calm the townspeople.

Chapter Twenty-Six

Vince had wasted no time in following Jack's instructions.

"Jack, come over to the community center."

"Will they string me up? Or like Hildy said, tar and feather me?"

"Don't worry. I've got the lynch mob under control, but you have to come. Bring Hildy with you."

"As a body guard?" This whole thing was completely out of hand. He should have gone to each person and quietly told them what was going to happen, although the usual way was through certified letters. He'd been turned inward in his own grief so long he'd forgotten how others must feel about things.

He collected Hildy and told her what Jack had said. "I'm hoping you've had some martial arts or boxing practice, Hildy," he told her as they drove across town. "I think Vince believes you'll protect me. Why else would he have told you to come?"

"Because I know the whole story, I suppose. I'm on your side now, remember?"

"One down, two hundred to go . . . and Merry."

"About that . . ." There was a twinkle in Hildy's eye and she dug a key out of her coat pocket. "Sometimes, when Merry is gone, I feed the pets and check the plants. I certainly didn't see any signs of life this afternoon, did you?"

Jack grinned at Hildy and silently gave thanks for her. "No, I didn't. And I tried very hard to find her."

"Do you think something is wrong?" Hildy raised her eyebrows anxiously.

"Could be."

"She was very upset last time I talked to her. Are you worried about her?"

"Very," Jack admitted with all truthfulness.

"Then maybe, when our meeting is over, I should go over and check on her."

"It might be a good idea." Hildy was a very good actress, Jack mused.

"And," Hildy said, smiling at her own cleverness, "you can come with me. In case she's fallen or something."

"I'd be happy to, anything for Merry."

"It's settled then?"

"Yes." Now he had a way into Merry's house—if he survived the next few minutes.

The crowd at the community center was restless. When Jack and Hildy entered, it quieted and then grew even louder.

It had no doubt been Hildy who had surprised them. The puzzled looks around the room told him that people didn't understand why Hildy was with this traitor— or whatever they thought he was.

As soon as they sat down, Vince started the meeting.

"I understand there has been some confusion about the letters many of you received today. It's important that Mr. Frost and I clarify for you what, exactly, the letter means."

Muttering came from all corners of the room.

"I assure you, there is no confusion or trouble intended." Then Vince told them of the wrongly recorded deeds and the need for the quiet title action to sort things out. He meticulously explained the process, and when he was done he nodded at Jack.

"Mr. Frost has some ideas about what should happen once the titles are cleared. I'd like him to tell you about that."

That was the very last thing Jack wanted to do, but he was trapped. Merry was hiding from him, a roomful of angry people was eyeballing him malevolently, and all he could think about was life without the woman he loved. Still, ever a professional, Jack gathered his wits and walked onto the stage where Vince was standing.

He looked at the gathering and saw such a range of emotions it took him by surprise—rage, hatred, confusion, disappointment, bewilderment, sorrow. He began to speak.

"I apologize for the confusion today. I have no devious plan for Frost. Until recently, I had no plan whatsoever because I didn't know what my non-business-savvy relatives had done.

"It appears my great-grandfather, who owned much of the land around Frost, allowed his friends to farm the land and keep the profits. They paid the property taxes and lived on his largesse. Still, his name was on the deeds. Somewhere along the line, errors were made and the following generations were led to believe that they owned the land, not my great-grandfather. When my father died recently, I discovered that I was heir to land in Minnesota. In an effort to untangle the titles, we discovered the recording errors and have made steps to correct them."

"Yeah, so? That still means you're planning to take away our land!" Harry Conner shouted.

"And our hometown!" That was Regina Olsdorf.

The worried muttering increased. Jack held up his hand. "Here's my plan: No one has to leave their home or the land they've been farming. Granted, we'll have to work out rental agreements with my cousins, but I plan to be more than fair. Your houses will be put in your own names. You will own your own homestead so no one will be put out. Most of my share of the inheritance will be given back to the people of Frost. Anyone who is living in a house I own can have it. Vince will take care of that. And what *is* Frost family property is considered businesses, and they will be deeded to the city to do with as they wish. I know it may not be what you want to hear, but it's the best I can do at the moment."

Jack scraped his fingers through his dark hair. "I want to work with you, not against you. Give us time to sort this out and feel free to ask Vince as many questions as you like." He heard Vince groan. Jack didn't care. It served him right for the trouble he'd gotten them into.

"One more thing. I apologize to everyone who's been hurt by this. That was not my intent. I mean to make it right."

The wind had been taken out of everyone's sails. Vince was busy answering questions, but much of the crowd faded away now that they were reassured he was not going to do something dreadful. Townspeople even came up and thanked him for giving Main Street to the city and for saying they would get to keep their houses free of charge.

Hildy walked up beside him. "Well, you dodged a bullet there."

"I may have, but I think the cannonball is still coming."

"Merry?"

"I've decided that if she won't come out of that house for me willingly, I'm not going to go in after her. If she trusts me so little that she believes I could toss people out of their homes, then we have no foundation for a marriage."

"So you asked her then?" Hildy smiled. That suffering look in her eyes was gone again.

"A lot of good it did me."

"Oh, I'm not so sure." Hildy's gaze fell on the last row of chairs at the back of the room.

Looking frail and teary, Merry sat with her coat clutched to her chest, misery oozing from every pore.

"How long has she been here?" he asked.

"She slipped in when Vince started talking. She hid in the shadows in the back for a while, listening."

"So she heard everything?"

"It would have been hard not to." Hildy patted his arm. "I'm going home now, Jack. You're on your own."

Slowly he made his way to the back of the room. Merry sat there shivering like a frightened rabbit. His heart nearly broke as he moved toward her. Jack spun a chair around so he could face her.

They sat in awkward silence until Merry broke the hush. "I'm not going to live in that house without paying you for it."

Jack's mouth dropped open.

"Here." She pulled a dollar bill out of her pocket and thrust it at him. "Don't say I don't pay my way, Mr. Jack Frost!"

"You mean . . ."

"I'm so sorry I didn't let you explain. You have every right to be upset with me. And though it breaks my heart, I even understand if you don't think we have enough trust in each other to make a marriage." Tears rolled from her eyes and down her cheeks. "I really didn't lose trust, Jack, but I couldn't make sense of it either. I needed to talk to God about it."

"What did He say?"

She hung her head. " 'I'll be there.' "

"What does that mean?" He took her hand and stroked the palm with his thumb.

"That if I never saw you again, He'd still be in my life. And if I did see you, He wouldn't leave me alone. I just knew that either way, God would support me." She smiled through the tears, a rainbow after a storm. "After that, everything in me screamed that I should go to you . . . and here I am."

It was as though he could see clear through her. She'd laid herself bare to him. She'd accept his decision, he, who didn't feel he even deserved a say after what had happened.

"I can't live without you," he said flatly. "You are the first sunshine I've had in my life since I was twelve years old. I won't go back to living in that half-dead place, Merry. You have to stay with me. Please?"

She touched his cheek so lovingly, so tenderly, that it was as if a butterfly had rested its wings there.

"I will, Jack. Forever and ever."

"Forever. That will have to do."

Epilogue

....

"You got your work done I see," Merry said brightly. On each hip, she carried a chubby baby with curly black hair and a thumb in its mouth.

Jack looked up at the trees with their brilliant yellows, vibrant oranges, and vivid reds. It was a perfect Minnesota fall day.

"It took Jack Frost quite a while to paint all those trees with frost, but I did a good job, don't you think?"

"Magnificent."

Jack took one of the babies from her. He held him up and stared into his eyes. "Hi, Jack Jr." The baby beamed at him. His father's attention was soon drawn to the other baby, who was holding out chubby hands to him. Jack handed the little boy back to Merry and took the girl.

"I wonder if my brother would mind if he knew I'd named a girl after him."

"From everything you've told me about him, I know he would have been pleased."

"I hope so. At least from now on I'll always associate the name Jamie with happy thoughts."

Merry put her hand to his cheek. "Have I told you lately how happy I am?"

"Not since this morning." He put his arm around her shoulders, and the babies gurgled to each other.

One of them spotted Peppy dashing across the yard, and suddenly they were both struggling to get out of their parents' arms. When they were put down, Peppy gave them each a proper face washing and flopped on the ground between them.

"Now I have another male that my dog and cat approve of." Merry tipped her face to the sun. "Plus, we have the perfect arrangement: October through January in Minnesota running the shop, and the rest of the time in California."

"Do you miss teaching school?"

Merry tipped her head toward the babies, who were stuffing their mouths with grass clippings. "I feel like I'm just getting started." She leaned down and emptied the two little mouths with her finger. "I wish your brother could have had children of his own. Maybe he would have had twins too."

"Maybe, but I think Jamie's carbon copy might be right here in Jack Jr." The child had already managed to refill his mouth with clippings.

Now that Jack had opened up, Merry was hearing derring-do tales about him and his twin nearly every day. She dropped to the grass with her children. "You are my hero, Jack. You've been very brave, and look how you've healed."

Jack lay down and rested his head in her lap, and the children began to crawl on him like ants at a picnic. "Not me. God. He's the greatest healer. He proved it with me."

Merry looked at the twins and her heart swelled with happiness. "And these two are just what the doctor ordered."

About the Author

....

 JUDY BAER is the author of more than eighty books in numerous genres: women's fiction, romance, young adult, and non-fiction. A winner of many awards including the Angel Award, she has also been a three-time finalist for the Romance Writers of America RITA Award.

Born and raised on the prairies of North Dakota, Judy is well acquainted with small-town life. She now lives in the Minneapolis/St. Paul area with her husband. She is the mother of two and stepmother of three.

POST CARD

Love Finds You

**Want a peek into local American life—past and present?
The *Love Finds You*™ series published by Summerside Press
features real towns and combines travel, romance,
and faith in one irresistible package!**

The novels in the series—uniquely titled after American towns with romantic or intriguing names—inspire romance and fun. Each fictional story draws on the compelling history or the unique character of a real place. Stories center on romances kindled in small towns, old loves lost and found again on the high plains, and new loves discovered at exciting vacation getaways. Be sure to catch them all!

NOW AVAILABLE

Love Finds You in Miracle, Kentucky
by Andrea Boeshaar
ISBN: 978-1-934770-37-5

*Love Finds You in
Snowball, Arkansas*
by Sandra D. Bricker
ISBN: 978-1-934770-45-0

Love Finds You in Romeo, Colorado
by Gwen Ford Faulkenberry
ISBN: 978-1-934770-46-7

*Love Finds You in
Valentine, Nebraska*
by Irene Brand
ISBN: 978-1-934770-38-2

Love Finds You in Humble, Texas
by Anita Higman
ISBN: 978-1-934770-61-0

*Love Finds You in
Last Chance, California*
by Miralee Ferrell
ISBN: 978-1-934770-39-9

*Love Finds You in
Maiden, North Carolina*
by Tamela Hancock Murray
ISBN: 978-1-934770-65-8

*Love Finds You in
Paradise, Pennsylvania*
by Loree Lough
ISBN: 978-1-934770-66-5

*Love Finds You in
Treasure Island, Florida*
by Debby Mayne
ISBN: 978-1-934770-80-1

Love Finds You in Liberty, Indiana
by Melanie Dobson
ISBN: 978-1-934770-74-0

Love Finds You in Revenge, Ohio
by Lisa Harris
ISBN: 978-1-934770-81-8

Love Finds You in Poetry, Texas
by Janice Hanna
ISBN: 978-1-935416-16-6

Love Finds You in
Sisters, Oregon
by Melody Carlson
ISBN: 978-1-935416-18-0

Love Finds You in Charm, Ohio
by Annalisa Daughety
ISBN: 978-1-935416-17-3

Love Finds You in
Bethlehem, New Hampshire
by Lauralee Bliss
ISBN: 978-1-935416-20-3

Love Finds You in
North Pole, Alaska
by Loree Lough
ISBN: 978-1-935416-19-7

Love Finds You in
Holiday, Florida
by Sandra D. Bricker
ISBN: 978-1-935416-25-8

Love Finds You in
Lonesome Prairie, Montana
by Tricia Goyer and Ocieanna Fleiss
ISBN: 978-1-935416-29-6

Love Finds You in Bridal
Veil, Oregon
by Miralee Ferrell
ISBN: 978-1-935416-63-0

Love Finds You in
Hershey, Pennsylvania
by Cerella D. Sechrist
ISBN: 978-1-935416-64-7

Love Finds You in
Homestead, Iowa
by Melanie Dobson
ISBN: 978-1-935416-66-1

Love Finds You in
Pendleton, Oregon
by Melody Carlson
ISBN: 978-1-935416-84-5

Love Finds You in
Golden, New Mexico
by Lena Nelson Dooley
ISBN: 978-1-935416-74-6

Love Finds You in
Lahaina, Hawaii
by Bodie Thoene
ISBN: 978-1-935416-78-4

Love Finds You in
Victory Heights, Washington
by Tricia Goyer and Ocieanna Fleiss
ISBN: 978-1-60936-000-9

Love Finds You in
Calico, California
by Elizabeth Ludwig
ISBN: 978-1-60936-001-6

Love Finds You in
Sugarcreek, Ohio
by Serena B. Miller
ISBN: 978-1-60936-002-3

Love Finds You in
Deadwood, South Dakota
by Tracey Cross
ISBN: 978-1-60936-003-0

Love Finds You in
Silver City, Idaho
by Janelle Mowery
ISBN: 978-1-60936-005-4

Love Finds You in
Carmel-by-the-Sea, California
by Sandra D. Bricker
ISBN: 978-1-60936-027-6

Love Finds You Under the Mistletoe
by Irene Brand and Anita Higman
ISBN: 978-1-60936-004-7

Love Finds You in Hope, Kansas
by Pamela Griffin
ISBN: 978-1-60936-007-8

*Love Finds You in
Sun Valley, Idaho*
by Angela Ruth
ISBN: 978-1-60936-008-5

*Love Finds You in
Camelot, Tennessee*
by Janice Hanna
ISBN: 978-1-935416-65-4

*Love Finds You in
Tombstone, Arizona*
by Miralee Ferrell
ISBN: 978-1-60936-104-4

*Love Finds You in
Martha's Vineyard, Massachusetts*
by Melody Carlson
ISBN: 978-1-60936-110-5

*Love Finds You in
Prince Edward Island, Canada*
by Susan Page Davis
ISBN: 978-1-60936-109-9

Love Finds You in Groom, Texas
by Janice Hanna
ISBN: 978-1-60936-006-1

Love Finds You in Amana, Iowa
by Melanie Dobson
ISBN: 978-1-60936-135-8

*Love Finds You in
Lancaster County, Pennsylvania*
by Annalisa Daughety
ISBN: 97-8-160936-212-6

*Love Finds You in
Branson, Missouri*
by Gwen Ford Faulkenberry
ISBN: 978-1-60936-191-4

*Love Finds You in
Sundance, Wyoming*
by Miralee Ferrell
ISBN: 978-1-60936-277-5

*Love Finds You on
Christmas Morning*
by Debby Mayne and Trish Perry
ISBN: 978-1-60936-193-8

*Love Finds You in Sunset
Beach, Hawaii*
by Robin Jones Gunn
ISBN: 978-1-60936-028-3

*Love Finds You in
Nazareth, Pennsylvania*
by Melanie Dobson
ISBN: 97-8-160936-194-5

*Love Finds You in
Annapolis, Maryland*
by Roseanna M. White
ISBN: 978-1-60936-313-0

*Love Finds You in
Folly Beach, South Carolina*
by Loree Lough
ISBN: 97-8-160936-214-0

*Love Finds You in
New Orleans, Louisiana*
by Christa Allan
ISBN: 978-1-60936-591-2

*Love Finds You in
Wildrose, North Dakota*
by Tracey Bateman
ISBN: 978-1-60936-592-9

*Love Finds You in
Daisy, Oklahoma*
by Janice Hanna
ISBN: 978-1-60936-593-6

*Love Finds You in
Sunflower, Kansas*
by Pamela Tracy
ISBN: 978-1-60936-594-3

*Love Finds You in Mackinac
Island, Michigan*
by Melanie Dobson
ISBN: 978-1-60936-640-7

*Love Finds You
at Home for Christmas*
by Annalisa Daughety and
Gwen Ford Faulkenberry
ISBN: 978-1-60936-687-2

*Love Finds You in
Glacier Bay, Alaska*
by Tricia Goyer and Ocieanna Fleiss
ISBN: 978-1-60936-569-1

*Love Finds You in Lake
Geneva, Wisconsin*
by Pamela S. Meyers
ISBN: 978-1-60936-769-5

*Love Finds You in the
City at Christmas*
by Ruth Logan Herne
and Anna Schmidt
ISBN: 978-0-8249-3436-1

*Love Finds You in
Frost, Minnesota*
by Judy Baer
ISBN: 978-0-8249-3435-4

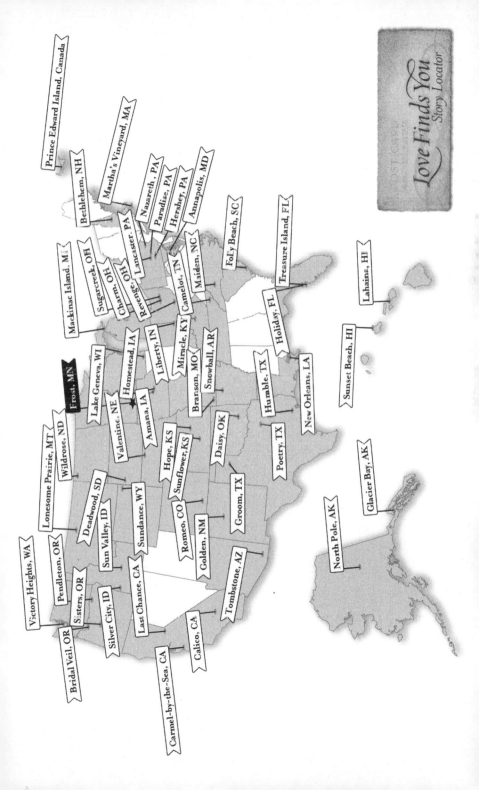

Love Finds You
Story Locator

Prince Edward Island, Canada
Bethlehem, NH
Martha's Vineyard, MA
Nazareth, PA
Paradise, PA
Lancaster, PA
Hershey, PA
Annapolis, MD
Folly Beach, SC
Treasure Island, FL
Lahaina, HI
Sunset Beach, HI
Mackinac Island, MI
Sugarcreek, OH
Charm, OH
Revenge, OH
Camelot, TN
Maiden, NC
Holiday, FL
Lake Geneva, WI
Liberty, IN
Miracle, KY
Branson, MO
Snowball, AR
Humble, TX
New Orleans, LA
Frost, MN
Homestead, IA
Amana, IA
Valentine, NE
Hope, KS
Sunflower, KS
Daisy, OK
Poetry, TX
Lonesome Prairie, MT
Wildrose, ND
Deadwood, SD
Sundance, WY
Romeo, CO
Groom, TX
Victory Heights, WA
Pendleton, OR
Sun Valley, ID
Golden, NM
Glacier Bay, AK
Sisters, OR
Silver City, ID
Last Chance, CA
Tombstone, AZ
North Pole, AK
Bridal Veil, OR
Calico, CA
Carmel-by-the-Sea, CA